# JANICE THOMPSON

## Spring Creek Bride

Steeple
Hill®

Published by Steeple Hill Books™

STEEPLE HILL BOOKS

Steeple
Hill®

Recycling programs
for this product may
not exist in your area.

ISBN-13: 978-0-373-82810-4
ISBN-10:    0-373-82810-1

SPRING CREEK BRIDE

www.SteepleHill.com

**Printed in U.S.A.**

# Ida couldn't seem to move.

In fact, she could scarcely breathe as she took him in. Funny, standing here in this close proximity, he didn't look like the criminal sort at all. But you could never tell with wolves, especially those so carefully disguised. She was a strong woman. She could overlook his attractions with little trouble.

Couldn't she?

"I don't believe we've officially met," Mick said.

"I know who you are, Mr. Bradley," Ida replied.

"And you are?" he asked, extending his hand.

Ida didn't want to answer his question, and yet her hand clasped his and her mouth spoke the words. "Ida Mueller."

"It's a real pleasure, Miss Mueller," he said, tipping his hat and holding on to her hand. For a moment, she was lost in his gray eyes, until Sophie cleared her throat, reminding Ida of her manners.

She quickly removed her hand from his.

## JANICE THOMPSON

is a Christian freelance author and a native Texan. She resides in Spring, Texas, near her grown children and infant granddaughters. Her family is active in ministry, primarily writing, music, drama and evangelism. Janice started penning books at a young age, and was blessed to have a screenplay produced in the early 80s. From there, she went on to write several large-scale musicals. Currently, she has published more than thirty full-length novels and nonfiction books (most lighthearted and/or wedding themed). She's thankful for her calling as an author of Christian fiction and knows the Lord has brought her to this point so that she can present stories that will change people's lives. Romances come naturally to Janice, since she's coordinated nearly a dozen weddings, including recent ceremonies and receptions for all four of her daughters.

Who knows whether you have come to
the kingdom for such a time as this?

—*Esther* 4:14

In memory of my father, Billy Hanna—
a small-town man with a big-as-Texas heart.

## Acknowledgments

To my agent, Chip MacGregor: You are a godsend.
Thanks for believing in me and special thanks for
finding just the right house for this story.

To Krista Stroever: Thank you so much for the
opportunity to write for Steeple Hill Books.
You helped make a long-term dream come true.
I appreciate your patience with the process.
You're a true mentor.

To Louise Rozett, my line editor: Thanks for the
spit-shine. You walked me through my first
copy edit at a new company, and I'm so grateful.

To my wonderful critique partners,
Kathleen Y'Barbo, Martha Rogers, Marcia Gruver
and Linda Kozar: Thanks for falling in love
with my hometown of Spring, Texas, with me!
Here's to lunch at Wunsche Brothers Café!
Let's meet there again…soon!

To the people of Spring, Texas (past and present):
You have left your mark on my soul.

# Chapter One

*Spring Creek, Texas, 1902*

Ida Mueller pressed a lock of unruly hair behind her ear and rounded the large dining table with a chipped serving bowl in hand. Chair legs scraped against the wood-planked floor as the rowdy lumber-mill workers rushed to sit down for another one of her home-cooked meals. She couldn't help but smile at their enthusiasm.

"Smells good enough to eat!" one of the younger fellows joked.

Ida plopped a spoonful of crisp fried potatoes onto his plate and kept moving as she responded. "You've eaten at my table every day for nearly a year, Carl Walken, and you haven't found reason to complain yet." She reached up with the back of her hand and wiped a bit of perspiration from her brow.

His eyebrows lifted mischievously. "Ain't just the food keeps me coming back." A playful wink followed.

"Ya reckon?" Another of the men elbowed him.

Several of the fellows let out whistles and Ida felt her cheeks turn warm. She scurried to the opposite side of the room and continued on with the chore of feeding the work crew, trying to ignore their usual flirtatious ways.

"None of that now." Her father's stern voice rang out from the head of the table. He always knew how to keep his men in line, especially when it came to his daughter.

"Aw, Mr. Mueller," one of the fellows groaned. "You never let us have any fun."

"Better mind your p's and q's," Ida quipped. "I've got a platter of Wiener schnitzel in the kitchen, but I've half a mind not to serve it."

The men took to hearty grumbling and she returned to the kitchen for the cumbersome platter of meat. For a moment—just a moment—she leaned against the countertop and drew in a deep breath. The south Texas heat wrapped itself around her like a dressing gown.

On days like this, she missed her mama more than ever. Seven years as the woman of the house had scarcely proven Ida worthy of filling her mother's shoes. Papa offered plenty of encouragement, but she struggled daily to keep up with caring for her home, her father and a crew of ravenous workers. And she fought to overcome the grief of losing the one person a girl depended on above all others—her mother. Oh, how she longed for what she could not have.

"I need you, Mama," she whispered. Indeed, at nineteen, Ida found herself in need of a great many things that only a mother could offer. But she had to rely on Papa's manly advice, and cope with the ever-present teasing from the lumber-mill workers, a daily reminder that she, a lone female, resided in a world of men.

"Mama, I don't know how you did it." She whispered the familiar words as she snatched up the plate full of Wiener schnitzel and headed back into the dining room once again.

As she came around the corner, Ida caught a glimpse of her uncontrollable blond hair in the elegant carved mirror that hung above the buffet. Frustrated, she reminded herself to deal with it after feeding the crew. How any of the men could find her attractive was a mystery, to her way of thinking.

Aunt Dinah would never let her hear the end of it if she didn't start taking better care of herself. Ever the proper lady, Ida's best friend and confidant was of the notion that a woman should be able to handle a full day's work, a brisk walk to town to help tend the family store and an hour's Bible reading in the evenings, with time left over for necessary grooming. All in the hopes of acquiring the one thing Ida wasn't sure she wanted—a husband.

Ida remained convinced she would never find a man who even came close to the one she held in the highest esteem—her papa. He was strong spirited, full of goodness and had a heart like a jewel. No, surely such a fellow did not exist. And if he did, he certainly didn't appear to be seated at this table.

"Thinkin' I'm hungry?" Carl asked. Ida looked down, shocked to see that she had placed five large slabs of veal steak on his plate.

"Oh, dear."

Her father's eyebrows arched as if to ask, *Where is your head today, daughter?*

She lifted three of the pieces of meat from Carl's plate. "I knew you had a taste for my cooking, is all."

With fork in one hand and knife in the other, the young man dove into the food. The others followed suit and the air soon filled with the sounds of chomping and cutting.

Her father cleared his throat quite loudly and Ida anticipated his next words.

"I don't believe we've thanked the Almighty yet." His voice deepened in reverence. "So you'll be putting down those utensils, gentlemen, or there will be no dinner for you today. Or any other day, for that matter."

They complied with sheepish grins, as always.

Ida noticed that her father's German accent became stronger as his prayer began. "Almighty God, Maker of heaven and earth, we thank Thee for this, Thy bounty. For Thy goodness is everlasting, from generation to generation, and Thy blessings overflow. Be with each of these men today as they seek to serve Thee with their labors. Amen."

"Amen," the men echoed, then tore into their food once again.

Ida slipped away into the kitchen, anxious for another moment's peace. Perhaps here she could think clearly. Once the dishes were done, of course.

She worked at a steady pace, allowing her thoughts to drift until a familiar shrill whistle signaled a train's arrival. The afternoon run from Fort Worth came like clockwork at one-thirty, just as she finished the dishes. Some things could be depended on.

Others could not.

Mick Bradley peered out of the grimy train window and took in his first glimpse of Spring Creek, Texas. Not quite what he had pictured and a sure sight hotter. He pulled a handkerchief from his pocket and dragged it across the back of his neck to remove the moisture. No point arriving in town looking like a vagabond. Not with so much at stake.

As the train crawled into the station, the porter approached, pocket watch in hand. "Just a few more minutes, sir."

Mick nodded in his direction, but said nothing as he took in the sights of his new home. Off in the distance a large hotel with a freshly painted sign greeted him. Sellers Hotel. And to his right, The Harvey House. After locating a barbershop, he'd have to settle on one or the other.

A bustling mercantile appeared to be doing quite a good business. Shoppers scurried to and fro with packages, stirring up dust on the street. A couple of women were about, but for the most part, he only saw men. Hundreds of men.

Yes, the booming little town of Spring Creek must surely need his services.

Mick's brow furrowed as he counted the saloons. He strained to see a bit farther down the street. Three? In such a small area? Their owners would be a source of contention, no doubt. Surely they would seek to complicate his plans to build a new gambling hall.

But he had encountered plenty of trouble when he opened his first place up North. These Texans couldn't be any worse than Chicago's most notorious, whom he'd handled with ease.

At that moment, two men took to brawling in the middle of the street, not twenty feet from the jailhouse. The taller, more muscular man clearly had the upper hand. A crowd gathered round, cheering them on. Before long, the two were on the ground, tussling. They went at it, cheek to fist, until one of them was knocked out. With such a large group about, Mick couldn't tell which one had taken the fall, but it must surely be the smaller of the two. That's how life was, after all. The boisterous crowd thinned as it declared a victor and the short man stood and raised his fist in the air with a triumphant shout.

Maybe these Texans weren't going to be so easy after all.

The passenger in the seat next to him stood and gave a polite nod as the train came to a stop. Mick returned the gesture and rose to his feet. His back ached from sitting so long and his cramped legs begged for a good, long walk. How many trains had he boarded over the past several days? Somewhere between Illinois and Texas he'd simply lost count.

The next few months would give him plenty of opportunity to stay put, however. He had his work cut out for him. And before long, he would be the talk of the town.

Probably sooner rather than later.

## Chapter Two

The afternoon journey to town provided Ida with an opportunity to think about the day ahead. She didn't mind the walk, though the late-spring heat continued to fold her in its sticky embrace. Her skirts, dusty and ragged on the ends, twisted about her ankles as she moved along the tiny, jutted road that connected the lumber mill with Midway, the town's main street.

She looked both ways before crossing the tracks, contemplating the barreling locomotives and the havoc they'd brought with them. Somehow it all seemed exaggerated in the heat. She tugged at the neckline of her dress, and a trickle of perspiration rolled down her back.

Surely Aunt Dinah would scold Ida for her appearance. Ah, well. Nothing Ida could do about that. Nor did she care to. If living among men gave her a tomboyish appearance, so be it. There were worse things, to be sure.

As she made her way from the tracks to town, Ida struggled with the usual attentions from the railroad men. Many let out a whoop or a holler as she passed by The Harvey House, and still more as she eased her way past Sellers Hotel, which happened to be known for a bit more than rooms to let.

As was her custom, she ignored the men, keeping her mouth shut to avoid giving them a serious tongue-lashing. She would gladly tromp through mud, splashing dirt upon her gingham skirt if she thought it would cause them to turn their irksome attentions elsewhere. Let her hair remain mussed. Perhaps then they would focus on their work and not on her.

"Come on, Ida," one of the fellows chided. "Just one glimpse into those perty blue eyes. They melt me like fresh-churned butter."

She kept her eyes on the ground and continued walking. The irritating fellow reeked of alcohol and pipe tobacco, and his work clothes were in serious need of washing. His scent, coupled with the over-powering smells coming from the nearby livery stable, almost brought her stomach up into her throat. Add to this the foul odor from the outhouses and the lingering stench of cigar smoke and one could scarcely stand it.

Yet this seemed to be her lot in life. Ida longed for a quieter, more genteel existence that did not include such aromas. If only Spring Creek could return to its former state—a quaint town with good, wholesome neighbors who greeted one another with pleasant hellos.

"C'mon, honey," the man pleaded, oblivious to her thoughts. "Can't ya give me a wink or somethin'? Some sign that I stand a chance with ya? I'll die if you don't." An exaggerated groan followed, one meant to get the attention of others nearby.

She willed herself not to look up. Why encourage him?

"Aw, yer killin' me." He doubled over and fell onto the road, eliciting a roar of laughter from the other men.

Ida managed to maintain her sense of dignity and simply kept walking.

She made the turn onto Midway and peered up long enough to gauge the distance. If she could just make it beyond the Wunsche Brothers saloon, the jailhouse, the barbershop and the bank, she'd be fine. *I can do this.*

A minute later, she reached the overgrown lot next to the mercantile and breathed a sigh of relief. Just twenty more paces and she'd be in the store. Dinah would be waiting, as always. Probably with pursed lips, but waiting, nonetheless.

The clock above the bank sounded two piercing gongs. *Why is it I can never arrive at a place on time?*

Ida picked up the pace and ran head-on into one of the men. With her cheeks flaming, she looked up at the fellow, ready to give him a piece of her mind for not watching where he was going. Why were these railroad men so careless?

Words failed Ida as she took in the handsome stranger with his polished good looks. She'd certainly never seen a man like this before, with such a finely tuned air about him.

Tall and sturdy, the stranger wore a fancy suit and big-city shoes—no cowboy boots like the rest of the fellows. His expression gave the appearance of dignity and confidence, unlike so many of the railroad men. Surely this man didn't work for the Great Northern, though he'd likely traveled in style aboard one of the nicer cars, from the looks of him. Yes, this was a man with money.

Perhaps he was a banker. Or better yet, a preacher, come to convince the wayward menfolk they were in need of repentance. Then again, he could be a socialite, headed toward the Houston area. Many well-mannered men had passed through Spring Creek on their way to other locations. Oh, if only they would stay and put down roots. They would balance out the bad with some good.

"Pardon me, miss." The gentleman spoke with a deep, rich voice. He tipped his hat, all politeness and charm, then gave a gracious bow. "My fault entirely."

Ida stammered in response, mumbling a few twisted-up words that amounted to little more than gibberish. He gave her a curious look and paused, likely to see if she might try again.

Ida managed, "Oh no, please don't apologize. I take the blame solely upon myself." She felt the heat rise to her cheeks as she spoke, noting his remarkable gray eyes. Remembering her manners, she quickly added, "I am sorry. I didn't mean to run you down." His sandy-colored curls drew her eye up. My, but he was a tall fellow. Stately, even.

He flashed a warm smile. "Oh, you can run me down anytime you like."

Stifling a smile, she shifted her gaze to his tailored suit and spiffed-up shoes. In all her years, she'd never seen a man with such a handsome wardrobe. Only in catalogs had she seen such finery. Up close, it was a little intimidating.

"Pleasure to meet you."

"And you," she managed.

"Have a good day." He gave her a nod then began to move in the direction of the barbershop. Ida watched as he disappeared through the crowd.

One of the railroad men shouted, startling her. "Ida, sweet pea, you're the woman of my dreams."

"More likely the woman of your nightmares, if you don't back away and let me pass," she muttered under her breath.

Shaking her head, she plowed forward. Four paces. Three. Two. One. Ida crossed over the threshold of the mercantile and let out a huge sigh of relief. Now, if she could just keep her mind off handsome strangers and on her work, all would be well.

Mick eased his hat back onto his head and continued across the street, ignoring the magnetic pull of the petite blonde. His heart had quickened at the sight of her, likely the result of her undeniable beauty. He was taken with her simple, small-town appeal, her flushed cheeks and determined expression—all things he loved in a woman.

And spunk. Yes, he could read the spunk in those flashing blue eyes, eyes whose image would linger in his mind for quite some time.

Mick quickly reminded himself of his reason for coming to Spring Creek. Not to find a woman, but to build a gambling hall. They were two very different things. Best to stay focused on the task at hand. After all, he had his investors to answer to.

Then again, he would need the help of the local women, wouldn't he? Yes, he would surely need barmaids and dancers. However, the woman he'd just fixed in his mind looked like the sort who was more at home on a church pew than a bar stool. If all the women of Spring Creek were like the one he'd just met, he'd have to look elsewhere for employees.

But he suspected that the blue-eyed beauty who'd practically run him down was one of a kind. One of a kind indeed.

## Chapter Three

Ida entered the mercantile at exactly five minutes past two. She slipped on her apron and started arranging canned goods.

"Well, it's about time."

Ida's brow wrinkled in concern as she heard Dinah's voice. She looked up, seeing the strong family resemblance in her aunt's stern eyes. Papa and his younger sister bore the same features, without question. And they had similar temperaments, as well, despite their vast difference in age. Dinah was a mere twenty-eight, though her mannerisms often led folks to believe otherwise.

Dinah had suffered much over the past couple of years and the cares of life had aged her somehow. But since the death of Dinah's husband, the family had grown closer than ever and Ida treasured her friendship. Papa had taken his only sister and her son under his wing, caring for their every need. No one could doubt his generous nature or his kind heart. And that

very kindness had prompted him to purchase the mercantile and place it into Dinah's capable hands last fall.

"Because I know you will do it right," he had proclaimed. "You will make the Mueller family proud."

And indeed she had. Nestled amid saloons and
restaurants, the store remained the town's last sensible place, where folks could come to share a good
story, purchase life's necessities and hear Dinah's
ardent presentation of God's love. The shop stayed
full from morning till night with those hungry for
companionship and direction.

And Ida, always ready to lend a hand, came every
day at two o'clock to spend time behind the counter so
that Dinah could focus on Carter, her five-year-old son.

Only two o'clock never seemed to come at the
right time, particularly not on days like today with
so many chores to be done.

"I'm sorry I'm late. Really, I am." With a gesture
toward the street, Ida added, "But this time I have
an excuse. I wasn't watching where I was going and
I ran right into this man. He was... It's hard to
describe. He wore the most beautiful clothes. He
must have just arrived on the train. Funny—I didn't
even get his name."

Dinah gave her an inquisitive look. "Why, Ida, I
don't think I've ever seen this side of you. You're
smitten."

Dinah's comment startled Ida. She tried to busy
herself arranging jars of honey. "I would hardly call
it that. I'm simply curious." She paused to think

about her aunt's words before adding, "It's just that he's so different from all the other fellas. Those railroad men are…they're impossible. This stranger was a true gentleman." She put down the jar and looked out the window at a couple of men who'd taken to scuffling with each other in the street.

"Are they still giving you a hard time on your trip to town?" Dinah picked up a broom, as if ready to do business with anyone who dared to enter in a flirtatious state of mind.

"Yes." Ida's dander rose as she revisited the trip down Midway. "Our little town is looking more like Houston every day. Railroad men. Taverns. Primitive behavior in the streets. The place is losing its innocence, which is why it's so refreshing to see a man of refinement for a change. I do hope he's here to stay, and not just passing through on his way to Houston."

"Most of the strangers who come to Spring Creek do not come with the best of motives." Dinah crossed her arms at her chest, looking more concerned than ever.

"Oh, I know." A sigh escaped Ida's lips as she reflected on the problem their town now faced. "And you can be sure the afternoon train brought in more riffraff. Every day they come, headed to the land agent's office to buy up their piece of the pie. The town is growing up too fast. It's frightening." She felt a little shiver run up her spine.

"At least business is good." Dinah gestured to the cash register with a smile. "I sold several pounds of coffee this morning. And there's not enough chewing tobacco in the state to keep these men happy." She paused a moment as she gazed around the very busy shop. "Best of all, they pay cash." She lowered her voice to a whisper. "Unlike so many of the locals. I can't tell you how many of them buy on credit and then don't pay their bills on time. It's a problem, Ida."

"I know, but—"

"I've traded some of my best merchandise for butter, eggs, herbs, even chickens," Dinah said with exasperation. "And then there's Mrs. Gertsch! Would you believe the woman actually wanted to trade in a stack of her used dime novels for honey?"

Ida couldn't help but chuckle at that news. After all, she'd sold the elderly woman those dime novels in the first place—they'd spent hours discussing the adventure stories. But this might not be the best time to share that information with Dinah.

"I'm not saying I mind so much," her aunt continued, "but cash money is a good thing for a business."

"Still," Ida argued, "I'll take a hardworking local over a cash-handling railroad man any day to make the town safe again. It's hardly worth risking life and limb just to get down Midway. Whatever happened to our sleepy little town?"

"Woke up, I guess." Dinah took to sweeping the floor.

"Humph." Ida shook her head in defiance. "I'd give my eye teeth for a return to the way things used to be."

She continued to look out the window, trying with

all her might to remember the little town that had captivated her heart when she was a child. In her mind's eye, she saw what Spring Creek would be like now, if the railroad had never come through. She saw churches, fields of sugarcane and delightful little shops. Women and children walked about in safety, packages in their arms and carefree smiles on their faces. Men gestured kindly to one another, never shouting obscenities, and never, ever whistling at women. In that quaint place, people would feel safe, secure.

Dinah's son, Carter, bounded into the room, breaking into Ida's thoughts. Jam stains covered his face, from brow to chin.

"Son, what have you done?" Setting the broom aside, Dinah rushed to his side and pried the jar of homemade strawberry preserves from his tightly clenched fist.

"Mine, Mother." He grinned with mischief in his eyes. Though Ida knew he deserved a good scolding, she had to stifle a laugh.

"At two o'clock in the afternoon?" Dinah asked as she placed the sticky jar on the countertop. "You believe this to be the proper time for sweets?"

"Anytime is the proper time, so long as it tastes good. Right, darlin'?" Ida scooped her young cousin into her arms and spun in circles until they were both dizzy. Carter let out a giggle, which bounced around the room and startled a few of the store's patrons.

Ida didn't mind a bit. In fact, she couldn't help but spoil this precious child, who was the spitting image of his father. Oh, if only Larson had lived to see his son grow up. If only that awful railroad man hadn't—

No, she would not focus on the family's losses today. Surely this blessed little boy was the good Lord's reminder to all who gazed upon his innocent face that life could go on, even after tragedy.

"Oh, fine." Dinah shook her head. "You're a big help."

"I know, I know." Ida carried Carter to the back of the store where she located a rag and some lye soap. "Give us a minute for a Texas spit-shine, and we'll be as good as new!" she hollered.

She gave the youngster a good scrubbing. He fought her attempts, but only in fun. When they finished, she led him by the hand through the carefully organized aisles of dry goods up to the front, where Dinah stood waiting, hands on her hips.

"See?" Ida grinned. "Cleaner'n a whistle."

Carter skipped behind the front counter and eyed the candy jars. "Jelly beans, Mommy?" he begged.

"No, son. I think you've had enough treats for one day."

"Peppermint?" He pointed to a second jar.

"Absolutely not."

Ida stepped in front of the row of glass jars so they would present no further temptation. Surely he would be pleading for licorice whips or gum before long. Or taffy. He loved the colorful, hand-wrapped delicacies from nearby Galveston Island.

Safely distracted, Carter grabbed his bag of brightly

colored marbles. As he settled onto the floor to play, the bag spilled open and they rolled around in every direction, making all sorts of racket against the wood-planked floorboards.

"Peawee, Mother!" he hollered, then dashed underneath the counter to capture his favorite marble in his tight little fist. "Peawee!" he said again, holding it up.

Dinah sighed as she reached to pick up the other wayward marbles.

"The only problem I see with boys," Ida said with a wink, "is that they grow into men." She joined Dinah behind the counter in preparation for the usual midafternoon influx of customers.

"You'd best not carry on with that train of thought," Dinah said, "or you will never catch a husband."

Ida rolled her eyes as she responded, "I'm not looking for one, I assure you." Before she could stop it, an image of the handsome stranger floated through her mind. She quickly pushed it away, determined to remain focused. Sensible girls were not swayed by fancy clothes.

She thought of her childhood friend, Sophie Weimer, who had no greater wish than to marry and present her husband with a half-dozen children in steady succession. Ida shuddered at the very thought of such a life. No, she would not marry—at least not unless the Lord presented her with exactly the right man. And she wasn't likely to stumble across the right man in a place like Spring Creek.

At that moment, a couple of rough-looking rail-road fellows made an entrance. They jabbed one another in the ribs and let out simultaneous whistles in the direction of the ladies.

"None of that in here." Dinah faced them, brow furrowed, ready for a battle. "Or you'll have me to contend with."

Their gazes shifted to the floor and they wandered off to play dominoes, pulling wooden-slatted chairs around a barrel and settling in for a game. The men-folk often gathered in the store to pass the time this way. No wagering, of course—Dinah would never abide such a thing.

Ida didn't mind their presence in the store so much, as long as they kept their language clean. And they were better off here than in the saloons, after all. There was nothing wrong with an innocent game of dominoes.

"I wish I had your patience." Ida spoke to Dinah in a hoarse whisper. "Truly. I can't seem to look a man in the eye without wanting to slap him."

Dinah gave her a sad smile. "That's because you haven't yet loved a man."

Ida nodded, as if Dinah's words settled the matter, but a feeling of uneasiness settled over her. Love did not carry the same appeal for her that it did for others. It almost seemed to be more trouble than it was worth. "I could happily live my whole life without knowing what that feels like."

"Oh, my dear," Dinah said, turning to face her. "I

predict you will one day look a man directly in the eye and slapping him will be the furthest thing from your mind."

Mick managed to locate the barbershop in short order and entered to the sound of raucous laughter from the patrons inside. The barber, an elderly fellow with smiling eyes, introduced himself as Orin Lemm, a native of Spring Creek. His assistant, a young fellow named Georg, ushered Mick to a chair and promptly took to lathering up his whiskery chin, a minty smell filling the air.

"Work for the railroad?" Orin asked as he finished shaving a man in the chair next to Mick's.

Mick guarded his answers. "I'm from the Chicago area. Just visiting." There would be plenty of time to explain his reason for being here later on.

"Really?" Orin's face lit up. "I have a cousin who lives in Sha-ka-gee. Maybe you know 'im." He dove into a monologue about his cousin's liver condition, scarcely pausing for breath.

Once Mick was lathered and ready, Orin moved over to take Georg's place. As the older man worked the razor this way and that, he continued to talk nonstop. His knowledge of Spring Creek was clear, and his pride in the town surely exceeded that of anyone else. In fact, Mick couldn't remember when he'd ever heard someone brag to such a degree.

"Spring Creek was just a tiny place when I was a boy," Orin explained with great zeal. "Mostly farm-land."

"Oh?" Mick found that hard to believe, consider-ing the current state of the town. How long had it been since the hotels and stores had been built? Likely they'd come about as a result of the influx of railroad workers.

"Yep. Sugarcane and cotton," Orin continued. "But when the railroad came through, everything changed overnight. Much of the land was acquired by the railroad. We're a major switchyard for the Great Northern now. Fourteen lines of track and a roundhouse."

"Not everyone's happy about that," one of the railroad men interjected. "Folks 'round here've made me feel about as welcome as a skunk at a picnic."

Several of the others made similar comments, though most agreed they'd grown to love the area, in spite of the heat and the poor reception from the locals. Mick wondered how they'd stopped perspir-ing long enough to fall in love with the place.

"I've got no complaints," Orin was quick to throw in. "Having you men in town has really helped my business. Never seen so many whiskers in all my days. And life's not boring. That's for sure."

His young assistant nodded in agreement. "You won't hear me complaining."

Orin proceeded to fill Mick's ears with all sorts of town gossip, covering everything from who was bickering with whom to where to buy the best liquor. He thought the whiskey at the new Wunsche Brothers Saloon was the best around.

And he discussed, in great detail, the shapely legs of the dancing girls at the town's most notable saloon, The Golden Spike. This certainly got Mick's attention, though not because of the women who worked there or their legs. Any saloon, notable or otherwise, would soon pale in comparison to his gambling hall. If everything went according to plan, anyway.

On and on Orin went, discussing the exceptionally warm weather and the cost of a meal at The Harvey House, a place he heartily recommended, especially on the nights when Myrtle Mae was cooking. Whoever she was.

Orin snipped away, shifting his conversation to the women in the town. "Not many to be had," he commented, "so I hope you haven't come with hopes of finding a wife like the rest of these fellers."

"The thought never crossed my mind." Though appealing women back home had drawn his eye, he'd never spent enough time with any one of them to be tempted. Not that he had any negative feelings regarding marriage in general.

No, Mick had no bias against matrimony. And he had nothing against the women in Texas, either, for that matter. He'd already taken note of at least one lovely female. His thoughts shifted to the beautiful blonde he'd just met. Why hadn't he asked her name?

Well, no matter. In a town this size, surely someone would know her. He would have no trouble giving an accurate description, having memorized every detail, from the wild hair swept up off her neck, to the blue eyes, to the determination in her step.

The barber finished up his work, and Mick stood to leave. His cheeks stung from the brush of the razor strokes and the pungent smell of the lather lingered in the air. He rubbed his palm across his smooth chin and smiled at the older man. "Thanks so much."

"My pleasure."

Mick dropped a couple of coins into Orin's hand and turned to leave. Exhaustion washed over him. He needed to locate a quiet room for the days ahead, a place where he could sleep off the train trip and begin to sort things out.

After a few paces, he found himself in front of The Harvey House. From what he'd been told, it was the nicest place in town. Hopefully, it would turn out to be the quietest, too. He'd check in first, then visit the local mercantile to make a couple of necessary purchases, then get some much-needed sleep.

Holding back an escaping yawn, Mick climbed the steps to the hotel, wishing a rainstorm would come along to wash away the sticky south Texas heat. He stood atop the steps and turned to look out over the little town. He couldn't quite put his finger on it, but Mick actually felt the definite stirrings of a storm ahead. Only this one likely had nothing to do with the weather.

# Chapter Four

Ida tended to the shop throughout the afternoon. Seemed no matter how hard she worked, she could scarcely find space enough for all the goods. Every square inch of the mercantile was stacked high with barrels, boxes and bins, from front to back. It always seemed to be this way when the season changed. The goods in the store shifted to accommodate seasonal needs.

With time, Ida managed to make sense of it all, but not without a considerable amount of strategy on her part. Boxes of summer goods were emptied, jars and bins were stacked and spring items that hadn't yet sold were placed on a sale table.

As she worked, the locals came and went—many making purchases, others just passing the time. Ida swept the wood-planked floor, and then began the arduous task of dusting the upper shelves that housed the store's finer merchandise, above the pine showcase. She smiled as she studied the handiwork of the showcases, which held higher-priced glassware. They ran the entire length of the store, from back to front. Papa had worked for weeks on the detailing, and it showed.

After dusting the shelves, Ida opened a showcase and repositioned the china dolls inside. Why in the world Dinah would stock such delicate items in a town like this remained a mystery. Ida had never asked, wondering if perhaps Dinah secretly longed for a daughter, someone who might play with beautiful dolls like these. Regardless, these breakable beauties would likely never sell in a town like Spring Creek.

Ida turned her attention to a hand-painted porcelain washbowl and pitcher. It reminded her of the one her mother had used each morning. Determined not to grow sad, Ida forced the memory from her mind. Only hard work could head off a somber attitude and with the heat hanging so heavily in the air, she could scarcely imagine adding a sour disposition to an already difficult day.

A few minutes before four, the brother of her friend Sophie entered the mercantile, red-faced and clearly upset. Ida didn't intentionally listen to Eugene Weimer's dissertation, but his booming voice rang out across the store, leaving her little choice.

"Just came from the barbershop," he explained in a huff. "A big-city fella in a fancy suit and hat rode in on the afternoon train from Chicago. Really tall fella. Maybe ya seen 'im."

Ida stopped what she was doing. She knew exactly who Eugene was talking about.

"Chicago?" several of the men echoed. One mumbled "Yankee" under his breath.

Ida hadn't considered the fact that the man might be from up North. Still, she couldn't imagine why that would make much of a difference these days.

"What's he doing here?" one of the fellas asked, his eyes flashing with anger.

"That's the problem," Eugene said. "No one seems to know. But be sure he doesn't look like one of us. Mighty suspicious to me."

"Traveling salesman?" another man asked.

Ida secretly hoped the man didn't turn out to be of that particular occupation. Traveling salesmen had poor reputations, at least the ones who'd dared show their faces and their wares around these parts. They were often ushered onboard the next train out of Spring Creek. And Ida was never sad to see them go. They stole business from the mercantile, after all, and their highly touted products usually left much to be desired.

Eugene shook his head and shoved his thumbs into his belt loops. "He was traveling light, from what I could tell, so I doubt he's selling anything. But my gut tells me he's got a story to tell, and it ain't a good one."

"Likely he has family in the area is all," Ida said with a shrug, unable to resist joining the conversation. How dare they judge the man without even knowing him! Didn't they know the Bible spoke against such things?

"Nope," Eugene said. "Orin weaseled that much out of him. He's got no people here. And he don't work for the railroad, neither."

"Hope he ain't come to Spring Creek lookin' fer a wife!" one of the men hollered out. "He'll have to get in line. And if'n he tries to cut in front of me, I'll take him down in a minute!"

Ida held her tongue, though it took every ounce of strength to do so. If he had come looking for a wife, he'd jump to the head of the line simply because of his genteel nature and fashionable attire, no doubt about that.

Eugene folded his arms at his chest and shook his head. "I'm guessing he's here to buy up land, not fetch a wife."

"I heard someone bought the Salyer farm," Ida interjected. "Maybe he's the new owner." Yes, an explanation like that would make perfect sense, wouldn't it? Purchasing a local farm wouldn't make him suspect, by any stretch of the imagination.

"He don't look like any farmer I ever saw," Eugene said. "Dressed all uppity-like. And his shoes—never seen a shine like that on any man's feet. I could almost see myself in 'em."

"Hmm." Ida knew the men would find this the most suspicious evidence of all. Every man in Spring Creek wore boots—nothing but.

"What kind of a fella would show up in a place like this, wearing slick, show-offish shoes?" one of the older men grumbled.

Eugene leaned in to the crowd and spoke in a strained voice. "I'm guessin' he's here to buy up our local businesses and take over the town. It's been happening all over the state—not just in Spring Creek. Yankees movin' in and buyin' up shops and mills on the sly whilst the locals are lookin' the other way. I'd wager he's a sly one, and well trained at that."

"Well, we ain't gonna let him get away with it," one of the fellows hollered out.

"We've had enough of that," another added.

Eugene squared his shoulders and added his final thoughts on the matter. "The whole thing just gripes my gizzard. I've had enough of folks sweeping in and taking over." He began to list all the times such a thing had happened, and Ida sighed. She couldn't argue the point. Spring Creek had been taken over by out-of-towners, after all.

"What is this man's name?" she asked when Eugene finished.

"Bradley." Eugene's eyes held a gleam of suspicion. "Mick Bradley."

"Did someone call my name?"

The crowd grew silent and a parting of the waters seemed to take place as Mick made his way through the throng. Ida kept her distance, just in case the men got riled up.

"Someone got something to say to me?" Mick asked as he looked around at the crowd.

No one uttered a word, and the beating of Ida's heart seemed to drown out everything else for a moment.

Even though he might have come to town to create trouble, she still found him an inordinately handsome man. With a fresh, clean-shaven face, no less.

*Focus, Ida.*

Nothing in the fellow's air spoke of ill will for the people of Spring Creek. Surely the others were wrong about him. Likely, he would turn out to be the new owner of the Salyer farm, was all. And, if so, she would take over a pecan pie once he got settled in. Just to be neighborly, of course.

Just then he looked her way and they exchanged a glance. She couldn't help but notice the pleased look in his eye when he saw her. She tried not to react, but the edges of her lips betrayed her. Ida swallowed hard, trying to maintain her composure.

When no one responded to Mick's question, he tipped his hat and went on about his business looking over the items on the shelves. He asked Ida to help him with a toothbrush and tooth powder. A feeling of contentment washed over her. *See there. He's well groomed in every conceivable respect. And he didn't come in to purchase chewing tobacco, like most of the other men. No, this one is certainly different from the others.*

Ida waited on Mick at the register, ignoring the whispers and stares of the others in the room.

When he left the store, another lively conversation erupted. Ida did her best to ignore it, though she was as intrigued by Mick Bradley as they were. But she was hoping for the best, while they were expecting the worst. Would he be good for Spring Creek, or bad? Ida didn't know, but she was sure of one thing— she would take a dozen Mick Bradleys over those foolish railroad men any day.

As Mick made his way across the street to the hotel, he thought about the reception he'd just received in the mercantile. Just the little bit of conversation he'd overheard while entering the store had been enough to convince him of their distrust. But what had he done to prompt such a reaction? What motivated such a hard and swift judgment on their part?

His suit, maybe? Some of the fellas had seemed to give him a once-over, taking in his clothes. Sure, most of the Spring Creek men were dressed in more casual attire. But a man's suit shouldn't make him suspect, should it? A few men had looked at his feet. So what if he opted for shoes over boots? Nothing odd about that, at least where he hailed from. Were Texans always this skittish as far as Northerners were concerned?

Mick tugged at his collar and willed the heat to go away as he entered his room. How in the world would he stand this? Surely in this sort of heat, the pine trees must be whistling for the dogs.

Why had he come to Spring Creek again? From his second-story window at The Harvey House, the town didn't seem terribly impressive, at least not in comparison to Chicago.

*Well, that's why I'm here. To make it impressive.*

He chuckled as he lay down on the bed, remembering the greeting he'd received at the front desk when he'd checked in earlier.

"You ain't from 'round here, are ya?" the clerk had asked.

"No, sir. I'm from the Windy City."

"Amarillo?"

Mick couldn't help but laugh. The fellow had looked a bit miffed.

He certainly wasn't making a lot of friends here in Spring Creek.

Maybe, as Orin had suggested at the barbershop, the local men feared he'd come to town to find a wife. Mick found himself smiling as he thought about the blonde. What a lucky coincidence to see her again. And luckier still that he'd learned where he could find her on a regular basis. She'd given him an impish smile, one that made him want to visit the mercantile again soon.

Well, no matter, Mick thought as his eyes began to close. He shook off any ill-conceived notions of courting her or any other woman in the near future. No, he'd better keep his head on straight while he was in Spring Creek. Otherwise someone might just come along and knock it off.

# Chapter Five

Mick's stomach rumbled for the umpteenth time. Now that he'd had a good rest, he was ready for a meal. The smells coming from the kitchen caused his stomach to leap as he entered the dining room. *Wonderful, blessed food.* How long had it been since he'd had a meal in a room that wasn't rocking back and forth as he ate, the clacking of train wheels reverberating in his aching ears? Too long.

He glanced around the noisy room. Dozens of men, mostly railroad workers, he would guess, filled the place. He couldn't help but notice their inquisitive stares, their eyes filled with distrust. Had the rumors of his presence spread that quickly?

He observed his prospective patrons. He'd seen worse than this scraggly bunch. Before long, these fellas would be his allies.

Mick soon found himself seated across the table from a stern-looking older man with a broad cigar hanging from his lips. Unlike the others in the room, he was dressed well. Surely he didn't work for the Great Northern.

"Cain't say as I've seen you 'round these here parts," the fellow quipped, the lit cigar jumping up and down as he spoke.

Mick nodded. "New to the area."

"Come in on the afternoon train?"

"Yes, sir."

The man gave him a pensive look. "Don't look like the other railroad fellas." He paused for closer inspection. "There's something different about you."

*I was just thinking the same of you.*

"Ah. Well, that's because I don't work for the railroad." Mick hoped the conversation would shift in another direction.

At that moment, the waitress appeared with a menu in hand. Mick quickly ordered the largest steak in the place, along with sliced potatoes and a huge piece of apple pie.

His dining companion made introductions, though the look in his eye did little to make a stranger feel welcome. "Name's Chuck Brewster."

"Mick Bradley." He extended his hand and gave the fellow a hearty handshake, then turned his attention to a glass of sweet tea.

For the better part of the meal, Mick avoided the older man's probing questions. Brewster could be a local businessman sniffing out competition. Or maybe he worked for the law. When Mick asked him a question or two, Brewster was as cagey as Mick had been about answering. For sure, he had something up his sleeve.

Mick left the restaurant at a quarter after six with a very full stomach, surprised to see the sun only just leaning toward the western sky. The slight oranges and reds ran together, casting a colorful haze across the street. For half a minute, the town almost looked presentable. He pulled a map from his pocket and began to walk in the direction of the property where his new facility would go up, passing the land agent's office on the way. He'd have to stop by first thing in the morning to seal the deal. After that, nothing could stop him.

He located the lot in question, and found it to be an overgrown field next door to the mercantile—a ragged piece of property at best.

Mick looked it over with a careful eye. A considerable amount of work would need to be done before any building could begin, but at least the patch of land was strategically nestled between the bank and the mercantile, perched and ready for notoriety. In his mind's eye, Mick saw the place—roulette wheels spinning, cards slapping against tables, glasses filled with alcohol, barmaids laughing, the heady scent of tobacco hovering in the air…

Only one thing seemed poised to get in his way. He turned and looked directly across the street at Spring Creek's largest—and from all rumors most notorious—saloon. The Golden Spike. The name shimmered in lights above the doorway. And standing just beneath the glittering letters was a familiar man with a lit cigar dangling from his lips.

With a silent nod in Chuck Brewster's direction, Mick turned and headed back toward the hotel.

## Chapter Six

The late-May sunshine rippled through the trees, causing the pine needles overhead to glisten like an emerald-green parasol. Ida wound her way beyond the gristmill, through the comfort of the familiar forest, and entered the clearing to the west of Spring Creek's tiny schoolhouse. The rustic wood-framed building hadn't changed much over the years. Indeed, it had remained every bit the same since Ida's childhood days.

Standing there brought a rush of warmth to her soul, and memories surfaced. She saw herself as a little girl once more, rolling hoops with a stick across the schoolhouse yard. Pigtails bounced about on her head, and gingham skirts twisted around her ankles, just as they did now. Oh, the joy of those days! What sweet and simple times she had known as a child in this blessed place. What innocence and wonder.

Immediately, a dark cloud hovered over her reminiscing. Would the few children who remained in

Spring Creek fare as well? How could they, with the town on such a downward spiral?

Ida's thoughts shifted to a conversation she'd had with Papa just that morning, a most revealing chat about Mick Bradley, the handsome stranger in the fine suit. Unfortunately, he was not the man of integrity she'd made him out to be in her imagination. No, his intentions were clearly of another nature altogether. According to Papa, who'd heard it from the sheriff, Mick Bradley had come to Spring Creek to build a gambling hall.

Ida trembled with fury at the very idea. Didn't the townspeople have enough trouble with Chuck Brewster and his house of ill repute? And weren't there two other such establishments in town already— places where the railroad men and all those who were just passing through could get liquored up and wreak havoc? Did they really need another?

No indeed. And now that she knew the truth, Ida would do everything she could to stop Mick Bradley in his tracks before he brought more pain and corruption to her town. With determination taking hold, she resolved to do all she could to dissuade him from his task.

Just one small piece of business to take care of first.

Ida made her way across the schoolyard. The pungent scent of gardenias filled the air, the bushes nearly bursting with excitement. She remembered the day they were planted, just six years ago. Her teacher, Miss Marta, had thought it a lovely idea to offer the children a flower garden of their very own.

Of course, Miss Marta was Mrs. Hollander now. She had long since married and moved on to Houston, like so many others. But the flowers remained a testament that things of strength continued to blossom and grow, in spite of adversity.

Was Spring Creek strong enough to keep blooming with so many villains about? And how could she, a simple girl, accomplish the kinds of changes she sought? Only one way. She must seek out help—and she knew just where to begin.

Ida tiptoed a bit closer and squinted in an attempt to see through the classroom window. The boys and girls squirmed at their desks. With school letting out in less than a week, they were likely to be anxious for a romp in the sunshine.

Sophie Weimer, her dearest childhood friend, stood at the front of the classroom looking quite scholarly as she gave the children their assignments. Her shirtwaist showed off a tiny waist, and her broad skirt swished this way and that as she tended to the needs of her students with great enthusiasm and a broad smile.

"It's a shame you're only filling in until a real teacher can be found," Ida whispered as she watched her friend at work. "You're quite good at this." She tugged at her collar, trying to gain some relief from the heat. "Come on, Sophie. It's time to ring the bell. Let 'em go."

As if she had somehow heard Ida's thoughts, Sophie reached for the bell on her desk and dismissed the students for the day.

Out they flowed, like tumbleweeds rolling across a plain. Little Maggie Jordan shrugged off the attentions of one of the boys—a bully by the name of Everett. Several of the lads raced from tree to tree. Ida watched them all with amazement. How long had it been since she and Sophie had run from that same door, headed out to pick dewberries? And how many years had it been since she'd worn her braids twisted up on her head like so many of these little darlings?

Ida walked up the steps to the schoolroom and peeked inside, taking in the familiar desks and inkwells.

A smiled broadened her friend's face. "What brings you to our schoolhouse this afternoon?" Sophie asked.

Ida pressed a hair behind her ear and gave Sophie a knowing look. "I've come to see what kind of a teacher you make."

"I've heard from the students that I make a fine one," Sophie said with a laugh. "Of course, I also made a fine waitress for The Harvey House, and a fine worker at the gristmill before that. And I can shoe a horse with the best of 'em. Any other questions?"

"I dare say, you excel at everything," Ida said with a nod, "which is exactly why I've come to ask your opinion on something."

"What is it?"

"I've come to speak with you about a matter of

utmost importance to our community," Ida stressed. "Something I believe you will find *very* troubling."

"Ah. I see." Sophie closed up the classroom and together she and Ida stepped out onto the playground, where several of the children were still gathered around.

"Run along home now, boys and girls," Sophie instructed. "I'm sure you've afternoon chores to get to. We don't want your parents to worry."

Everett let out a groan. "Aw, Miss Sophie, you're no fun."

"If they had any idea the kind of trouble you stirred up as a child," Ida muttered under her breath, "they might think otherwise."

Within a matter of minutes, the students had all scattered to the winds, their childish ramblings now just a whisper among the pines.

"You look as if you don't feel well," Sophie commented as they started on the path to town. "Has something happened?"

Ida sighed. "I'm afraid so." Pulling out a handkerchief, she swabbed the back of her neck to rid herself of the moisture underneath her hairline. "You know that piece of property next to the mercantile?" She folded the hankie and tucked it into her sleeve.

"Yes, of course."

"Any guesses as to who's bought it?"

Sophie spilled out a long list of names, and Ida shook her head with each one.

"Who, then?" Sophie asked.

They stopped walking and Ida looked Sophie in

the eye. "A stranger. From up North." She felt foolish as she realized how easily she'd been taken in by the man's polished exterior. Why, if not for the sheriff's conversation with Papa, she might very well have continued on with her fanciful notions about Mick Bradley. But no more. Now that she knew the truth, justice would surely follow.

Concern filled Sophie's eyes. "I'd been told that piece of property would be ideal for a new feed store. Mr. Skinner was looking into purchasing it, wasn't he?"

"That's not to be. Mrs. Skinner told Dinah that her husband is considering building on the outskirts of town to avoid the chaos on Midway, or perhaps abandoning the idea of a new store altogether."

"Can't say as I blame him."

"Me, either." Ida sighed again. "But there is more to the story."

"Do tell."

"I heard Papa talking to the sheriff, who stopped by our place just this morning. The new owner of the property next to the mercantile is a gambling-hall fellow from Chicago named Mick Bradley, come to bring more greed and despair to our town. He's going to open a place for the railroad men to load up on liquor and gamble their earnings away."

"No."

"Yes." Her anger intensified as she continued on. "And right next door to our store, no less. Can you imagine? Isn't it enough that we have to contend with the brawls from Chuck Brewster's place? And the Wunsche Brothers' saloon? The last thing we need is another such place."

Sophie paused, her brow furrowed. "This is a matter for prayer, Ida."

"Yes, of course. But don't you think the Lord would ask more of us?" Ida said as they continued to walk.

"More?"

"Someone has to *do* something," Ida implored. "We've watched and waited, prayed and pleaded, but things are only getting worse. It's time to grab the horse by the reins."

Sophie shook her head. "Oh, Ida. Have you talked to your papa about this? I can't imagine he would be happy to hear what you're saying. You know how he feels about your concerns."

"My papa is a strong man," she said. "And he has raised a strong daughter."

Sophie nodded. "To be sure."

They rounded the corner onto Midway, where activity abounded. Ida clamped her handkerchief over her nose as the overwhelming scent of horse manure assaulted her.

"Little good this does," she grumbled. The tiny square of cloth could do nothing to block out the mix of nauseating aromas—the ever-present stench of railroad men in need of a bath, the smell of soot from the nearby trains and the overwhelming scent of burnt grease from the restaurant at The Harvey House.

With great determination, she pulled the handkerchief away from her face and looked Sophie squarely in the eye. "I am on a mission," she stated quite plainly. "One from on high."

Sophie chuckled. "You have such a way of putting things, Ida. Perhaps you should be writing novels, not just reading them."

"I am quite serious, Sophie. Have you not read the book of Esther—in the Old Testament?"

"Of course I have." Sophie gave her a quizzical look. "But what does that have to do with you?"

"Esther was put upon the earth to save her people. The Bible says she was born for such a time as this. Remember?"

"Yes, of course. But—"

"I have no doubt that *I* was born for such a time as this," Ida explained, triumphant. "To save our little town from the evil influence of men like Mr. Bradley."

"Ah." A hint of a smile crossed her friend's face. "If I believed anyone were capable of saving our little town, it would be you."

"Truly?"

Sophie gave Ida a pensive look and arched an eyebrow. "You and the Lord working together, of course."

They stopped in front of The Golden Spike as Nellie DeVries, one of the dancing girls, sprinted past them in full regalia, almost knocking them down.

"Sorry!" the young woman called out with an apologetic giggle. "Chuck needs me inside."

Ida drew in a breath and kept walking. "This is just

the sort of thing that concerns me most, now that a new gambling hall might be opening up," she whispered. "Barmaids. Saloon dancers. The few women left in this town will eventually have little choice but to turn to occupations such as these."

"I do hope you're wrong." Sophie fanned herself.

Anger took hold again as Ida said, "What other choices will they have? All the reputable businesses will be gone, if these strangers have their way. And I, for one, won't have it. I will not allow the girls of Spring Creek to grow up into women such as…such as…" She pointed at the door that Nellie DeVries had just vanished behind and sputtered, "Women such as that!"

Sophie looked at Ida carefully. "Ida, perhaps you're judging a bit too—"

Ida never heard the rest. Her attentions shifted to Mick Bradley's property across the street. She gave it a stern once-over. "This is the spot where that good-for-nothing out-of-towner hopes to weave his web. And I plan to stop him in his tracks." Ida turned to look her friend in the eye. "I do need the Lord's help. But I've come to ask for someone else's assistance, as well."

Sophie's eyes lit with understanding. "Ah. You mean me."

"Indeed." Ida nodded, knowing Sophie would understand the depth of her meaning. "I mean you." She leaned in, and added, "Even Esther couldn't manage alone, you know."

Sophie linked arms with Ida. "In that case," she

said with a smile, "I am all yours. Someone's got to keep an eye on you, Ida Mueller," she teased. "At this rate, you're likely to set the entire town ablaze with your great passion for propriety."

Irritation set in as Mick gazed at his property. Only three days into his new venture and already his plan was fraught with problems. The land agent—the same one who had assured him by letter that the lot would be his as soon as money changed hands—had suddenly turned up with another offer. The scoundrel was probably just trying to up the ante, but Mick wasn't playing that game.

Still, he had come a long way, and for what? To lose the piece of property he'd been assured would be his? Could he risk that? What would the investors back in Chicago say?

Maybe he should up his offer, just to be safe.

On the other hand, folks weren't exactly warming up to him. The local sheriff, a burly fellow with an overgrown mustache, had paid a visit to his hotel room just last night. What was it he had said, again? Ah, yes. Something about making his visit to Texas brief. Not exactly a threat. More of a warning.

And the ever-present stares from the saloon owners—especially Chuck Brewster—who clearly saw him as a threat to their businesses, did little to calm Mick's troubled mind. How could he keep the peace and still get the job done?

Maybe he could convince the pretty blonde to help

people see him as the upstanding businessman he was. She probably knew everyone in town, since she worked at the mercantile. Perhaps he should pay her a visit and see if he could win another one of those lovely smiles. Purely for business reasons, of course.

# Chapter Seven

"You're late, Ida."

"I know, Dinah. I know." Ida flashed a sheepish grin as she slipped behind the mercantile counter. She busied herself refilling a jar with black licorice, avoiding her aunt's accusing glare.

"I'm partly to blame," Sophie added as she leaned her elbows on the countertop, a habit Ida knew Dinah disliked. "We got to talking and the time slipped away from us."

"Still," Dinah said, glancing at the clock and then at Ida with a look of frustration, "you are exceptionally late…even for you."

A guilty sigh escaped from Ida's lips. "I am sorry. Truly. But I needed to ask Sophie's opinion about the new gambling hall that's going in next door."

A couple of their regular customers passed by the counter, slowing as they heard mention of the gambling hall. Ida closed her mouth and continued on with her work, an act of penance.

"Ah." Dinah's eyes narrowed. "I see. And what does your friend have to say about this latest dilemma?"

"That it is a matter for prayer," Sophie said, looking at Ida.

"The Lord is calling us to action," Ida explained, "and I'm to lead the way." She contemplated delving into her story about Esther, but decided to keep it to herself for the moment.

"Oh?" Dinah raised an eyebrow.

"I've arranged a meeting with Reverend Langford tomorrow afternoon. He will know best how to advise me. And I am convinced he will agree that we cannot sit idly by with the enemy so clearly at work."

"Reverend Langford is a good man," Dinah agreed, "and a sensible one. He will give you a reasonable answer. He is not prone to violence, so he will respond with caution."

"I am not advocating violence, of course," Ida insisted. "But the Almighty expects his people to take action, to face their enemies with courage. Remember David and Goliath? Remember Shadrach, Meshach and Abednego?"

"Your second example bears little practical application, Ida," Dinah corrected, "but I can certainly see the resemblance between our situation and what young David went through as he faced the mighty giant. Perhaps we've a goliath of our own in this out-of-towner."

"Yes, that's it." Ida's heart quickened at the thought. "And the saloon owners want to see this latest one gone, as well. They're on our side for once."

Dinah crossed her arms. "I dare say the saloon owners make for somewhat strange and uncomfortable allies." She lowered her voice. "And I suspect they have their own reasons for wanting to see him gone."

"True," Sophie responded. "He will surely steal much of their business. That won't go over well."

Dinah drew in a deep breath and the look on her face grew more serious. "I hate to think of what will happen if they become angry. We will find them a force to be reckoned with, to be sure."

Ida could hardly imagine what sort of trouble the saloon owners would stir up, if crossed. She'd never thought about any of this from that angle before. Truly, she only wanted to stop Mick Bradley.

Carter interrupted their conversation as he scurried behind the counter, chattering merrily. He opened his palm and showed them several of his most colorful marbles, gabbing all the while about his favorites.

Ida reached down and lifted the tiniest one from his hand to serve as an illustration. "I might be small like David. But with just one little stone, I could take those giants down. I could take them *all* down!"

She looked up, triumphant. Immediately her heart plummeted. Directly across the counter stood Mick Bradley with an amused look on his face. The little marble slipped between her fingers and hit the floor, *plink-plinking* against the wood-planked floorboards as it rolled out of sight.

As they all stood in stunned silence, Ida wondered just how much the man had heard. Dinah finally came to her senses and gave him a welcoming smile. "Can I help you, sir?"

"Yes, please." He extended his hand, and Dinah gave it a shake. "I need to make a few purchases." He handed Dinah a list to be filled.

Dinah took to gathering the items, but Ida couldn't seem to move. In fact, she could scarcely breathe as she took him in. Funny, standing here in this close proximity, he didn't look like the criminal sort at all.

But you could never tell with wolves, especially those so carefully disguised. This one's smoky gray eyes were a distraction, that's all—like puffs of smoke from one of the passing locomotives. And his broad smile was clearly a well-rehearsed bit he'd learned somewhere up North. A true Texan could sense dishonesty, particularly in a Northerner. His sandy-colored curls caught her eye again, but she forced her attention elsewhere. She was a strong woman. She could overlook them with little trouble.

Couldn't she?

Mick flashed that practiced smile in Ida's direction and approached her.

"I don't believe we've officially met," he said.

"I know who you are, Mr. Bradley," Ida replied, trying to ignore the fact that she couldn't seem to overlook his handsome features after all. *No, I will not be taken in by this heathen from up North, this tool of the enemy come to bring corruption and vice.*

"And you are?" he asked, extending his hand.

Ida didn't want to answer his question, and yet her hand clasped his and her mouth spoke the words, "Ida Mueller."

"It's a real pleasure, Miss Mueller," he said, tipping his hat and holding on to her hand. For a moment, she was lost in his gray eyes, until Sophie cleared her throat, reminding Ida of her manners. She quickly removed her hand from his.

"This is Sophie Weimer, Mr. Bradley."

"Please, call me Mick. I'd appreciate it, ladies," he said, shaking Sophie's hand but keeping his eyes on Ida. Ida felt a flush rise in her cheeks, and she took Sophie by the arm, pulling her to the storeroom.

"Th-that's him?" her friend whispered, eyes wide. "Why, he's the handsomest thing I ever did see. Better than a picture in a book, to be sure. You forgot to mention that part, Ida!"

"Sophie," Ida whispered, "do not be deceived. This is not a man to be trifled with. He is evil through and through, despite his looks and fancy clothes. Besides, do you not remember what the Bible says? The enemy comes at us like a wolf in sheep's clothing." She turned back and gave Mick Bradley another look through the doorway. "He is on the prowl, even now."

Yes, that wolf of a man was certainly adorned in sheep's clothing. His fine gray suit. His shiny shoes. His stylish felt hat. In fact, she couldn't say when she'd seen a finer-looking sheep.

Sophie gave Mick a second glance. "There's no denying, he is the most handsome man I've ever set eyes on. I can't help but wonder if he's married."

"Sophie!" Ida shook her head in exasperation.

Dinah called out her name, and Ida left the storeroom with Sophie following on her heels. Ida turned and gave Sophie a stern look. "What's come over you?" she whispered. "You're acting like a smitten schoolgirl."

A slow smile spread across Sophie's face. "Why, Ida Mueller. I do believe you're jealous!"

"Jealous? How can you say such a thing?" Ida sputtered.

"I think I'm not the only one who's wondering if Mick Bradley is married."

"Don't be ridiculous," Ida said, reaching to straighten several bolts of fabric that were already straight. "And please wipe that annoying expression off your face."

Sophie tried to look serious. "Will this do?"

"Now that's the girl I know and love," Ida replied.

Sophie broke into laughter as Ida turned in a huff and joined Dinah to fill Mick's order with haste.


The dirt-streaked hotel room window provided Mick with a near-perfect view of the town. From here, he could almost see the sign on the front of the mercantile. Why he felt drawn to the place, he could not say. If anything, he should steer clear of it at all costs. The women inside that establishment clearly took issue with him, though they were all politeness and smiles during his visit. He sensed their concern and would do his best to put their minds at ease. No point in quarreling with the neighbors, after all, especially one with startling blue eyes, like Ida Mueller.

Mick was perplexed by the change he saw in her. Was it not just a few days ago she'd smiled at him in that particularly fetching way? Now, suddenly, she'd taken on a different attitude, one he didn't much care for. The way she'd said, "I know who you are, Mr. Bradley," was all business, and he'd opted not to ask for her help, as he'd originally planned. Maybe she'd discovered his reason for being here and had taken it as an affront.

Why he cared what she thought remained a mystery. They scarcely knew each other, after all. Still, from the moment of their first encounter, he'd locked those beautiful blue eyes into his memory.

"Stop it, man. Don't be thinking about a woman. You'll be back in Chicago before long and there are plenty of sensible—or not-so-sensible—women there to fill your thoughts."

Indeed, as soon as the gambling hall began to go up—he'd decided to call it The Lucky Penny—Mick would search out the perfect candidate to run the place in his stead, someone from his neck of the woods, most likely. If he selected a local for the job, the community would surely turn on the poor fellow; the whole thing might even end in bloodshed. No, he couldn't risk that. Wouldn't be good for business. It would have to be someone his investors approved of—someone with a head for numbers, a heart for turning a profit and big-city experience.

Shouts rang out and Mick turned his attention to the street below. Several of the railroad men had gathered there, instigating yet another fight. These Texans were certainly boisterous, and a sure sight more complicated than he'd figured. Prideful, to be sure. And standoffish. Maybe it had something to do with all the dust they swallowed as the trains barreled by. Clogged up their throats. Regardless, many of them had already voiced an opinion by refusing to do business with him. Pure stubbornness.

And then there was the issue with the property. According to the land agent, the owner—a man from the Houston area—was holding out for more money. Mick would pay it after all, just to get the game under way, though he hated to give in to such tactics.

He sighed as he thought about the situation. Really, what did it matter, when all was said and done? The payoff would be worth it. And he needed to get started on the building as soon as possible.

"Soon, fellas." He watched the brawling men as the quiet words slipped from his lips. "Soon you will have much more to do than duke it out in the streets. Soon you will be sitting at The Lucky Penny dropping all your hard-earned money into my lap."

If everything went as planned, the new building would be up before summer's end.

Mick used his sleeve to wipe the sweat from his

forehead. Troubling thoughts continued to plague him as he climbed into bed. He ached to shut the window, to drown out the whoops and hollers from below. Mick knew that many of the sounds came from The Golden Spike, just a few doors down, and that knowledge only added to his aggravation. Unfortunately, the heat simply wouldn't allow him to reclose the window. He shoved the pillow over his head in an attempt to silence the ever-present shouts and laughter of the men.

Out of the darkness, a shot rang out. Mick sprang out of the bed and raced toward the window, his heart pounding. With great relief, he saw that the sheriff had fired the shot into the air to send the men on their way. They scattered with little trouble, drifting off to the various hotels and boardinghouses.

Mick fell into bed a second time in a more hopeful state. Surely these Texans would eventually thank him for coming. Once The Lucky Penny opened, offering them more gambling opportunities, better liquor and a classier decor with a real stage for entertainment, Mike felt confident he'd be Spring Creek's new hero, if they'd just give him half a chance.

# Chapter Eight

The shrill whistle of the morning train from Galveston roused Ida from her groggy state. The grinding of brakes, the piercing squeal of metal against metal, the rhythmic clacking of wheels against lines of track—these familiar sounds at daybreak merged with the shouts of the railroad men as the cars inched their way by. *Why must we live so close to the switchyard?*

Papa had built the lumber mill years before the track was laid. But then the railroad had come through and taken over the town—in a hundred different ways.

Ida stretched for a moment and allowed her eyes to become accustomed to the sunlight peeking through the lace curtains. She propped up her pillows and sat up in the bed. Then Ida reached for the worn Bible on the bedside table, one of her most precious possessions, and ran her finger across her mother's name inside.

"Oh, Mama, I wish you were here." She missed

their morning prayers together and her mother's nightly readings from the worn book.

Ida leaned against the pillows and opened the Bible to the book of Esther, where she read, for the hundredth time, the story of the young queen approaching the king's throne with fear and trembling.

Ida closed her eyes, deep in thought. Every time she pictured Esther approaching the throne, she couldn't help but envision herself doing the same thing.

Oh, but what would it be like, to come into the king's chambers uninvited? To approach without invitation? And yet, Esther braved the journey, taking one courageous step after the other, and all because of God's calling—*for such a time as this.*

One step at a time, Ida saw herself inching toward the Savior's outstretched arms.

*Come to me, child. Don't be afraid.*

At some point along the way, fear gripped her heart and her eyes flew open.

"I am afraid," she whispered as she clutched the Bible to her chest, tears springing to her eyes. "I'm afraid I won't be able to do what You have called me to do. Or that I will somehow do it incorrectly. And I'm afraid—" she paused, startled by her thoughts "—that Papa will die someday, too, and I'll truly be alone."

She began to cry in earnest now. Where did this fear come from? Just because she'd lost her mother didn't mean Papa would soon follow.

She wiped her tears from her face. No, she wouldn't give herself over to mourning and fear—

not right now, anyway. Ida needed to be strong for her people. Esther wouldn't have given in to fear, would she? No, Esther was a woman of great strength, and Ida would be, too, regardless of the cost. She would meet with Reverend Langford today, as scheduled, and he would help her take a stand for the people of Spring Creek.

A rap at the door startled Ida back to her senses.

"Ida, are you all right? It's time to wash up and get started on breakfast." Her father's reassuring voice brought comfort. The sun now streamed in the window as reality set in. *I'm late.*

"I'll be there in a moment, Papa." She quickly got up and went to the washbasin to scrub the anxiety from her face. Her father would know. He always seemed to, though he rarely questioned her moods anymore. If anything, he simply left her to her ponderings and watched her out of the corner of his eye.

Ida scrambled into her dress and pulled her hair up into a messy knot on the top of her head. Another quick glance in the mirror gave her an opportunity to rehearse a smile, one she hoped to use on Papa as soon as they met in the kitchen. She knew he would be seated at the small table in the corner of the room, waiting for his coffee, ready to talk about what the day ahead held for them both. Hopeful and happy, as always. If only she had inherited that tendency.

She scurried down the stairs and into the spacious kitchen. True to form, Papa sat, spectacles perched on the tip of his nose, reading his Bible.

She forced the smile. "Morning, Papa."

Ida kissed him on his forehead and he reached to squeeze her hand. "Child, you're troubled this morning."

She tied an apron around her waist. "I'm fine. Truly."

"Humph." His eyes narrowed. "I've never known you to be dishonest, daughter."

Ida focused on the coffee, hoping to avoid his penetrating gaze. For some reason, she couldn't utter a word. Not over the lump in her throat, anyway.

He pushed his spectacles up. "Why not share what's in your heart? Don't you think it would make you feel better, after all?"

"I will, Papa," she assured him. She brushed tears from her eyes before facing him. "As soon as I'm ready."

With biscuits to knead, eggs to scramble and thick slices of ham to fry, she managed to avoid more conversation with her father. Thankfully.

At six forty-five sharp, a rap on the back door signaled the inevitable. Papa welcomed in ten hungry workmen. Their clothes, dingy and ragged, still carried the odors of a thousand yesterdays. How many times had she asked if she could launder their shirts and underclothes? Their pride appeared to be stronger than their noses, no question about that. And on this morning, she thanked the Lord for the smell of the food, which—at least temporarily—masked the stench of sweat and sawdust.

The men stampeded in, tramping mud all over her

once-clean kitchen floor. One by one they pulled off their hats, revealing hair in want of trimming. Why couldn't they take better care of themselves? Bathe once in a while? They could all take a lesson from Mick Bradley.

No. She would not think about him today. Pray for him, yes. Think about him, no.

"You've no manners a'tall," Ida scolded as the men guffawed and slapped one another on the back, paying no attention to her words. Nothing new there.

One of the fellows reached toward the platter of ham steaks on the countertop and snatched a loose piece with his fingertips. Ida slapped his hand. "Enough of that. Now get to the table, all of you. You'll be serving yourselves, today Plates are on the buffet, silverware and napkins in the drawer beneath." After giving instructions, Ida poured steaming cups of coffee for all, then retreated to the far side of the room as they bowed their heads for the morning blessing.

"I'll be in the kitchen if you need me," she explained afterward as they stared at her in confusion. Her father cast a curious glance from across the table and she offered up a weak smile. In truth, she simply needed to be alone with her thoughts. And the heat in this room, especially with so many pressed together, proved more than she could bear.

Ida went to work at once on the pots and pans. Her mind drifted to the man who so often captivated her thoughts of late. He'd surely made his presence known. At the mercantile. In the streets. And everywhere she turned.

The more she learned about Mick Bradley's shameful plans, the more she distrusted him. And the more she distrusted him, the stronger was her resolve to see him gone. Or to make him see the error of his ways.

To Ida's way of thinking, a man like Mick Bradley would be a tough sell to the Almighty. Pressing him through the pearly gates would take a bit more than Southern hospitality. It would truly take a miracle. Of course, the Lord was in the miracle-working business, but Ida still found it difficult to imagine.

She made up her mind to drop in on a few of the shopkeepers and encourage them to refuse his business. Of course, kindhearted Dinah would probably flinch at that idea. She tended to mix her faith with kindness, perhaps too much so.

*I'm not unkind—just firm.*

For a moment Ida reflected on the stubbornness she'd seen etched in Mick Bradley's handsome face. Ironically, it mirrored her own.

Regardless, she would teach him a thing or two about how to do business in Texas.

Mick breathed a sigh of relief as he left the land agent's office, the deal squared away once and for all. Now to begin the arduous task of clearing the land and purchasing lumber. He'd heard rumors about a lumber mill nearby. Surely that would be just the place to acquire all the pine he'd need.

Minutes later, as Mick neared the mill, a two-story house came into view. White with green shutters. Well maintained. Must be the lumber-mill owner's home. Should he knock on the door to inquire about purchasing lumber, or head around back to the mill?

Then, just as he drew near, the front door to the house swung open, and Ida Mueller appeared on the front porch with a bonnet in her hands. She scurried to close the door. In a hurry, as always.

He stood just yards away from her, close enough for his heart to nearly stop beating altogether. What was it about this woman? Why did he lose the ability to think clearly at the very sight of her?

"Miss Mueller." He removed his hat and flashed a smile, hoping she would return the gesture. When she did not, he popped the hat back into place and weighed his options. Common sense finally won out. He was here to do business, after all. "I've come to purchase some lumber."

"Oh?" She crossed her arms and gave him a curious look. From up there on the porch, her stern stance gave the illusion of height, though he calculated she couldn't be much more than five feet tall, at best. Still, her presence filled the porch.

"Yes," he replied. "Who would I speak to about that?"

"You would want my father." She nodded toward

the mill. "Though I can't imagine he will be selling you lumber today or any other day."

"Oh?" His smile faded. "And why is that?"

"Mr. Bradley, in case you haven't noticed, we're not keen on a gambling hall going up in town— we've got enough trouble with the saloons as it is. It's not likely my papa will lend his support to you or your establishment in any form or fashion."

The truth, at last. The reason for the coldness in her stare, the stiffness in her stance.

"But your father is a businessman. Surely he will see past any bias his daughter might have to sell me the lumber I need."

"I wouldn't count on it." Her blue eyes flashed with determination. "Though you are welcome to ask him yourself, of course. I was just headed into town for the afternoon to work at a reputable place of business."

The corners of his mouth turned up in amusement. "So you've taken on a job as barmaid at one of the saloons?"

Ida's hands went straight to her hips. "How dare you suggest such a thing? You take that back," she said angrily.

Disappointment washed over him—she'd found no humor in his joke. He wished he could indeed take his words back, but there was little he could do to remedy the situation now. "I'm sorry, Miss Mueller. I spoke in jest."

"There was nothing funny in what you said. Nothing at all."

"Again, I apologize." After a brief, awkward pause, he offered, "If you will wait until I'm done, I will escort you back to town."

Ida shook her head, slipping the bonnet over her blond curls and tying it at her chin. "That will not be necessary. I make the walk every day on my own, thank you kindly."

"But I've seen how the men jeer at you." He gave her what he hoped would be a fatherly look. "An escort would prevent that from happening, I assure you. Please wait for me."

Ida shook her head once more. "I would rather risk the jeers of a hundred railroad men than have a gambling-hall owner walk alongside me. And that is my final say on the matter." She marched down the steps with her chin jutted forward.

Mick stepped out of her way, realizing she would not be stopped. He followed her with his gaze until she made it to the street. Did she really consider him to be a bigger threat than the fellows who whooped and hollered as she walked by? Did she not recognize a true gentleman when she saw one?

Mick made his way around the house to the mill. Whether or not Ida's father would sell him the necessary lumber remained to be seen, but Mick wouldn't give up. No, he would proceed with his plans. And no one—not even feisty and determined Ida Mueller—would stop him.

# Chapter Nine

After a particularly long day, Ida arrived home to find Papa dressed in his Sunday best. She looked at him with curiosity as he straightened his tie, and asked the obvious question. "Going somewhere?"

"Into town for supper." He turned to her with a mischievous grin.

"But I'm planning to cook bratwurst. That's your favorite," she argued.

"It's pot roast and potatoes night down at The Harvey House," he said. "And Myrtle Mae has invited us to come for dinner."

"Myrtle Mae Jennings?"

Ida saw her father's thick mustache twitch a bit. That always meant a smile hid underneath.

"Papa?"

"What, Ida? Can't a man eat pot roast without a hundred questions from his daughter?" he asked, eyes twinkling.

"You can eat anything you like," she responded,

"but I suspect there is more to this story than meets the eye. Am I right?"

After clearing his throat, he offered up a vague answer. "Myrtle Mae is a fine woman." He glanced in the mirror to check his tie. "And a mighty fine cook."

"So am I," Ida said, hands on her hips.

Her father reached over and gave her a light peck on the cheek. "Yes, but we never know what the future holds."

"What are you saying?" She stared at him in disbelief. "Are you telling me I'm being traded in for someone who knows nothing about cooking German fare?" Her papa cut potential arguments short with a shake of his head.

"Daughter, I'm not trading you in or asking you to give up cooking. Trust me when I say I would never do that. I'm just in the mood for pot roast and potatoes, that's all."

"Sure you are."

"Now don't make more of this than need be. Come along and be a good girl now. Let your papa escort you to town for a nice dinner."

Her father headed toward the door, gesturing for her to follow. However, Ida stood with her feet planted firmly. Surely he must be joking. Why had he set his sights on Myrtle Mae Jennings, of all people? Everyone in town knew she was a busybody and, well, a chatterbox. Such a thing could hardly be tolerated in a woman.

On the other hand, perhaps Ida shouldn't judge too

harshly. Dinah had flat-out accused *her* of gossiping recently, with regard to Mick Bradley. But that was different, of course.

"Come, Ida. We are to arrive at six-thirty," her father said impatiently.

"But, Papa—"

"Come." He opened the door and extended his hand. She glanced in the mirror. "Can't I even have a minute to freshen up?"

"One minute." He gave her a wink. "I'll be on the porch swing, dreaming about that fine meal we're going to have."

"We could have had a fine meal at home," she muttered after he'd gone. However, after a long day of work, she might actually enjoy an evening of being waited on.

Even if it meant eating someone else's cooking.

Ida took advantage of her time alone to tuck some loose curls into place. And she couldn't very well go into the restaurant at The Harvey House wearing her dull brown gingham dress, could she? No, she might as well put on her Sunday blue with the puff sleeves. It wore well, and brought out the color in her eyes— or so she'd been told by Sophie, who knew more about fashion than anyone else in town.

As she dressed, Ida thought about the meeting she'd had with Reverend Langford earlier. He'd suggested they all do what they could to win Mick Bradley to the Lord. Not exactly the response she'd been hoping for. It seemed that no one was taking this gambling hall as seriously as Ida. She'd work to change that, surely.

Nearly fifteen minutes later, Ida made her appearance on the front porch. Papa started to scold her until he noticed her attire. "Why, Ida Mueller. I dare say you're as pretty as a field of bluebonnets."

"I'll take that as a compliment." She took his arm and together they made their way into town, talking all the way. Though she wished to avoid the subject of Mick Bradley, Ida could not. She found herself telling Papa everything she'd learned at the mercantile—how he planned to begin work on the gambling hall within days, and how he'd already hired men to clear the land.

Papa drew in a deep breath but did not respond, at least not at first. When he finally did speak, his words stopped her cold. "I did business with Mr. Bradley this very afternoon. Found him to be an amiable fellow."

"What do you mean?" She stopped and stared at her father, stunned. "Surely you did not sell the man lumber for that den of iniquity he is building."

"Daughter, I cannot control what people build with the lumber I sell them. Nor did the Lord tell me to avoid selling to him. This is not a matter of my linking arms with the man. I'm simply treating him with the courtesy I extend every customer."

"Papa." Ida shook her head, so upset she could barely speak. In her nineteen years she could not recall questioning any of her father's decisions. And yet, in one short day, he'd managed to arouse suspicions twice. Myrtle Mae and Mick Bradley? Had Papa lost his mind?

Pushing her misgivings aside, Ida entered the restaurant on her father's arm. The most wonderful aroma filled the air. Ida breathed it in, suddenly quite glad she had agreed to come.

She closed her eyes for a second. The noises in the room captivated her. The clinking of silverware and glasses. The sounds of waitresses bustling back and forth with their full skirts swishing this way and that. Boisterous laughter from a couple of men at a nearby table. Voices raised in conversation. The Harvey House was a lively place, no doubt about that.

She opened her eyes, noticing familiar faces in the crowd. To her great surprise, Sophie's entire family sat at a large table near the center of the room. The Weimer boys—Sophie's three older brothers—ate with gusto. And her parents looked up with matching smiles, motioning for Ida and her father to join them.

After taking her seat, Ida glanced at the menu, then turned her attention to the conversation at hand. The Weimers were talking about the upcoming church picnic on the Fourth of July, and the annual cobbler contest. She was about to express her desire to enter the contest this year when she spotted Mick Bradley at the restaurant door. Flustered, Ida tried to hide behind her menu.

"Is everything all right, daughter?" Papa asked, easing the menu down to look into her eyes.

"Oh, yes," she offered. "Everything just looks so good, I can hardly decide. I need to take a closer look." She peered up over the menu to look at Mr. Bradley once more.

"I'm having the pot roast," Papa announced to everyone within hearing distance.

"As you can see, so are we," Mrs. Weimer replied. "It's truly the best thing on the menu." As she sang Myrtle Mae Jennings's praises, Ida couldn't resist the temptation to groan.

"Are you all right?" Sophie gave her a curious look.

Just then Myrtle Mae entered the room with a broad smile on her face. She eased her ample frame through the crowd of tables, clapping her hands together when she saw Ida's father.

"Why, Dirk, I'm so happy to see you." Her cheeks, already flushed, deepened a shade as their eyes met. Ida took note, wondering when this attraction had begun. How had she missed it? And what could she do to keep it from going any further?

Her papa's mustache began to twitch at once. "After all I've heard about your pot roast, I wouldn't miss it." And then he winked at her.

Ida tried not to gasp aloud, but stifling her surprise proved difficult.

"What about you, Ida? What's your preference?" Sophie asked.

"My preference?" Ida stole another peek at Mick Bradley, who suddenly took notice of her. He gave her that smile and she felt her cheeks warm. Embarrassed, she pulled the menu back up. "I'm not sure what to order."

Sophie, puzzled by Ida's behavior, looked up and noticed Mick. "Well, you are certainly studying that menu," Sophie said with a hint of laughter in her voice. "You will have it memorized before long."

"Must be mighty hungry," Mr. Weimer added.

"More likely she can't find anything she likes," Papa interjected. "Ida has a tendency to prefer her own cooking over that of others."

"Oh, you really must try my pot roast, Ida." Myrtle Mae gave her a pat on the shoulder. "Perhaps I'll make a believer out of you," she said, smiling as she headed back to the kitchen.

Ida found it increasingly hard to concentrate, what with Mick Bradley standing directly across the room. Who could eat, when a man like that had just made his presence known?

Mick took a seat at a table well within view. For a brief moment, Ida actually felt sorry for the man, dining alone in a room full of strangers.

Sophie leaned over and whispered, "Perhaps we should ask the man to join us."

"Hush! He'll hear you," Ida replied.

Sophie laughed at Ida, and looked back at Mick. He raised his hand in greeting, and Sophie waved back. "He is one good-looking man, Ida. Surely looking at Mick Bradley gives you reason to rethink your position on marriage," she teased.

The only thing she wanted to rethink right now

was her decision to join her papa for dinner at The Harvey House in the first place.

Mick took note of Ida the moment he entered the restaurant. He couldn't help but notice her dressed like that. Nearly a dozen times during the meal he glanced her way, just to see if she would look back. He wanted to see how her eyes matched up against that beautiful blue dress. He imagined they'd knock him off his chair if he got a close enough look.

Unfortunately—or perhaps fortunately—that never happened. All too soon, Ida and her father left the restaurant with the group they'd been eating with. Mick had sensed her discomfort at his presence, and yet a wave of disappointment washed over him as she left.

On some level, Mick envied Ida, sitting with people she loved—in a group that size—to share a meal. He wondered if he'd ever know the love of a daughter, one who looked up at him with such awe. Or the admiration of sons, who hung on their father's every word like the trio of older boys sitting with Ida. Would he ever gather together with loved ones, praying over food as he'd heard them do, eating pot roast, and singing the cook's praises loud enough for all to hear?

For the first time in ages, Mick acknowledged that losing his parents twenty years before had left him with an emptiness inside. His brother had taken him in and fathered Mick as best he could, but he couldn't fill the void left by his parents. Watching Ida with her friends and family left him feeling lonelier than he'd ever felt in his life.

Would he ever again have a sense of wholeness— of family—like he'd had as a child before his parents passed away?

No. Likely he never would.

And the realization left a hole in his heart the size of Texas.

## Chapter Ten

Mick awoke the following morning with a splitting headache. He wasn't sure which had made it harder to sleep through the night—the ruffians in the street or the sounds of retching coming from the room next door. Regardless, he could scarcely function when the morning light streamed through the window of the hotel room.

He hadn't been able to stop the images of Ida Mueller in that blue dress—maybe that was the real reason he couldn't sleep. He'd wanted to catch a glimpse of her up close, but she'd walked right by him, never even looking his way. Had she done so on purpose, avoiding him deliberately?

He shook her out of his mind and sat up slowly. Plenty of work awaited him, and he needed to get to it.

He dressed quickly, and made his way out of the hotel and onto the street.

Ambling down Midway, he was amazed to find it nearly empty at this time of morning. Except for a few railroad men gathered at the station, the place was quiet. The morning dew left the first hint of a pleasant aroma in days. He paused for a moment, thinking perhaps he'd stumbled into a different world altogether.

At last, Mick came to the property. His patch of land. Within the hour, workers would begin to clear the spot. In his mind's eye, he could see how different the lot would look without the overgrowth of weeds. Come Monday, the foundation would be laid, and then the beams erected. Then the exterior walls would come together in no time at all.

Mick glanced over at the mercantile and saw Ida place the Open sign on the door. Their eyes met and he tried to read her expression. The hardness he'd sensed yesterday still remained. Surely there had to be more behind that look than his plans to build a gambling hall.

Mick's thoughts were interrupted by a child, probably four or five, running out the door with a puppy in his arms.

"Carter!" Ida scolded. "Your mama's told you a dozen times to keep that mongrel out back. She doesn't want you dragging him through the store."

"He's hungry, Ida." The pup wriggled loose from the little boy's grasp and ran out into the street.

Mick reached the squirming ball of fur just as it bounded onto his property. He walked to the mercantile and handed the pup to Ida with a smile. "I do believe this belongs to you."

"Thank you so much." He noted her attempt to muster up a stern look, but a hint of a smile took its place as the playful pup settled back into her arms. "We're so grateful."

"Puppy!" Carter took the little fur ball from Ida and headed back into the store.

"He's quite a handful," Ida said, "but the dearest thing in the world to me."

Mick looked away. His heart now rushed with a new emotion, one he'd never felt before. What would it feel like…what would it *be* like to have a woman like Ida to come home to? And a child?

Mick could hardly believe the thoughts that raced through his head. Men like him didn't marry, at least not until they were old or out of money. He had no real need for a wife. And she—whoever she was— would certainly not tolerate his desire to put finan- cial dealings before matters of the heart. No, family was not for him, no matter how lonely he'd been feeling lately.

He tipped his hat then turned back to his property, happy to get away from Ida Mueller and those blue, blue eyes that made him forget himself.

"Ida, I can't thank you enough for coming in on a Saturday morning." Dinah continued to fuss with her hair, then turned to Ida with a shrug. "How do I look?"

"Wonderful, but you're going to be late for the meeting."

With the wave of a hand, Dinah responded, "I

doubt Millie and Reverend Jake will care. We're just talking about the Fourth of July picnic is all. But they want to include me. They're always going out of their way to make me feel needed."

"They're not *making* you feel needed," Ida said. "You *are* needed. There is a difference. The reverend and Millie couldn't possibly pull off the annual picnic without your help, and you know it."

"Still," Dinah said, reaching for her bonnet, "I don't want anyone to feel compelled to include me." She gave Carter a kiss on the cheek. "Now, you be a good boy for Ida, son. Don't give her any trouble."

"No, ma'am."

"No, ma'am, you won't be a good boy, or no, ma'am, you won't give her any trouble?"

Carter giggled. "No, ma'am, I won't give her any trouble."

"That's my boy." Dinah patted him on the head, then turned back to Ida. "Thank you for minding the store. I'll be back before noon, I feel sure. And if you need anything—"

"Go, Dinah. Don't fret."

Her aunt drew in a deep breath, looking around the store, clearly anxious. "I forgot to mention there's a shipment of sugar due in and Mrs. Gertsch said she would be coming by to trade some items. Don't let her get away with too much, Ida. You know how she is."

"Yes." Ida tried to hide the smile.

"If her bartering goes on too long, she'll end up owning the store."

"I'll handle everything." Ida shooed her aunt out the door. "Now go on. How are Carter and I ever going to have any fun if you stay here?" Ida watched Dinah disappear down the street. Her heart secretly ached for Dinah. How such a dear, sweet woman could go on, day after day, after the tragedy she'd faced.

Ida shivered as she remembered that terrible night when Larson had leaped in front of an oncoming train to save the life of one of the railroad men, who was drunk on liquor purchased at Chuck Brewster's saloon.

He should have been the one to die, not Larson.

Ida drew in a deep breath, determined not to allow herself to focus on the past. If Dinah could move ahead, surely she could do the same. Carter needed them both to be strong.

Ida turned back to her cousin with a forced smile. "Would you like to play with your jacks while I'm tending to the cash register?"

"Yes, ma'am."

As she dusted the glass cases, Ida heard noise coming from next door. She looked out the window, stunned to see a crew of men working on the empty lot, clearing the weeds. Some of them were Papa's workers! Likely that scoundrel Bradley had offered them an exorbitant salary. What traitors! And Carl Walken, of all people. After all the food she'd served him, it seemed like a personal betrayal to find his feet planted in the enemy's camp.

Off in the distance, Mick Bradley spoke to one of the men, giving orders. Ida's skin began to crawl.

Imagine, putting up the gambling hall next door to a perfectly respectable general store where children played and folks gathered for decent conversation and honorable transactions.

The door opened and Sophie entered the store with her mother. She drew near to the register. "Did you see the goings-on next door?"

"How could I avoid it?"

"What are your thoughts?" Sophie leaned against the counter.

"I think they are making entirely too much racket for a Saturday morning. They are distracting my customers and that will soon affect my business."

Sophie looked around the empty mercantile. "Your business? But I don't see—"

"Exactly." Ida nodded as she yanked off her apron. "So, if you don't mind watching the register a few minutes, I'd like to go have a word with Mr. Bradley."

"Mind yourself, Ida," Sophie said with a smile. "Don't say anything you might regret later."

Ida gave her a look of warning and turned to catch her reflection in the glass case so she could tidy up her hair. No point in arguing with the neighbors with messy hair. She needed to put her best foot forward.

With nerves kicking in, she made her way to the door. One foot in front of the other. Then out onto the boardwalk. Then onto the street, nearing the spot where Mick stood in his high-falutin' shoes and dress coat, talking to Carl Walken, no less.

"Mr. Bradley!" Ida shouted to be heard above the noise of the workers clearing the lot.

He turned to her with a smile. "Lost that puppy again?"

"No." She shook her head, determined to keep her focus. "I am here with a complaint, one I hope you will take seriously."

"Oh?" His eyes twinkled with mischief. "And what sort of complaint would that be?"

"First of all, I feel compelled to tell you that the Bible strictly forbids gambling. For this one reason alone, I cannot bear to watch this building go up. And next door to a respectable business like the mercantile. Ridiculous!"

He opened his mouth to speak, but she forged ahead. "And one more thing." She pointed to his workers. "It's one thing to hire a man to do a job—it's another altogether to steal your workers from another man. These fellas work for my papa. They've got no business here in town working for you."

"Now hold on there, Miss Mueller. I haven't stolen anyone. These men are working on the weekend for extra cash—"

"Cash that will be spent in a saloon." She pointed to Chuck Brewster's place. "This is ill-gained profit, and you are behind it all."

"But I—"

"And have you not thought about the children of Spring Creek? No, you have not! I dare say, if you'd given one minute's thought to our children, you would realize that their innocence has already been assaulted. How will they ever remain pure and untouched by the vices of this world if a man such as yourself continues to build—" she sputtered the words "—a g-gambling hall!"

"Well, I—"

"And another thing!" She felt her courage rising. "I am accustomed to peace and quiet on Saturday mornings and so are my customers. With all the noise coming from your lot, the customers are staying away. We're losing business because of you."

"I would hardly think—"

"Now, my papa might not have been able to stand up to you, but I can. And will. And I can assure you, the saloon owners will stand up to you, too. There's not a one of them who's happy to see you here. Not a one. So I'd watch out if I were you, Mr. Bradley. I fear you may be taking your life in your hands if you continue building of this gambling hall of yours."

"Are you quite done?" he asked at last.

"I am." Ida was completely exhausted and shaking to the core. Still, she kept her hands firmly planted on her hips, and never let her gaze slip from his.

Mick let out a whistle. "Well, if that doesn't beat all!" After a chuckle, he added, "I do believe you've missed your calling, Miss Mueller."

"Oh?" She brushed a loose hair behind her ear, puzzled. She suddenly realized the men had stopped working so they could listen to her talking to Mick.

"If it's true that preaching is left only to the menfolk,

then the church has done you a great disservice," Mick announced. "Why, I can see you up there now, pounding your fist on the pulpit, shouting at the parishioners, pointing out the error of their ways."

A roar of laughter went up from the crowd of workers. A couple even slapped their knees. As a smile lit Bradley's face, she weighed her options. Fighting the temptation to do or say the wrong thing, Ida bit her lip until it nearly bled.

Clearly, the man refused to see the light. But he knew how to get his digs in, didn't he.

His expression softened a bit as he added, "Look. Don't you think I've got enough trouble from the men around here? Why would a pretty girl like you want to add to my grief? What have I ever done to hurt you?"

She began to tremble in anger. Why, if he didn't understand what he'd done to hurt her after all the time she'd just spent explaining, then he must be daft. Ida could hardly control her temper as she spouted, "You're…you're…impossible!"

She stomped her way back into the store, outraged and overwhelmed. No man had ever made her feel so…confused.

Sophie took one look at her and sighed. "Oh my goodness, Ida. Whatever happened out there?"

Ida couldn't answer at first. Speaking over the lump in her throat proved to be nearly impossible. Finally, she managed a few strained words. "He said I've missed my calling." She reached for her apron and, in her fervor, tied it a bit too tight. As she loosened it, she said, "According to Mick Bradley, I should have been a preacher."

Sophie laughed so hard she couldn't speak for a full minute. Then she said, "You know, he may have a point. You do have passion!"

"Sophie, I'm not looking for you to agree with the man."

"And you have a mighty fine vocabulary to boot! Not to mention the fact that you know the Bible stories inside and out!" Sophie collapsed in laughter again.

"Sophie, I thought you were in agreement with me about the gambling hall!"

"I am, Ida, of course I am. I'm sorry for laughing. I just think that Mick Bradley is impossible, don't you?" she asked.

Instead of replying, Ida reached for a broom and began to sweep—vigorously. Yes, Mick Bradley was impossible, all right. No question about that. So was her friend Sophie. Those two deserved each other.

The thought of Sophie and Mick together suddenly overwhelmed Ida with such jealousy she had to excuse herself and get her bearings. She had no idea what was happening to her, but she didn't like it at all. Not one bit.

## Chapter Eleven

Mick watched from a distance as the foundation was laid on his new property. He always loved this part, watching the concrete, soft and pliable, harden into something of great strength. He understood such a hardening—he had lived through it himself.

Some of the workers had questioned his use of concrete. Most of the buildings in the area had the usual pier-and-beam foundation. Still, Mick wanted to work with the latest technology, and a concrete slab was the way to go, from what he'd learned. Especially in a humid climate like this, where termites made regular appearances.

Not that he really minded what the locals thought about his decisions, anyway. They already considered him odd; the concrete had only served to reinforce that fact in their minds.

What mattered—what really mattered—were the opinions of his investors back in Chicago. They were the only ones he had to please. And surely they would agree with his choices. He needed to build a place that would withstand the elements and any other forces that might come along. The stronger, the better. He had a feeling the building would have to withstand some interesting challenges before all was said and done.

Mick allowed his gaze to shift to the mercantile next door. Several times he'd caught Ida peeking through the window, her interest in his business more than a passing fancy, no doubt. Once he'd even waved, just for fun. Naturally, she hadn't waved back.

Mick looked out over the lot once more. Tomorrow morning, the framework of the building would go up. And though he'd hired a perfectly fine contractor, Mick would be right here, watching every move the builders made.

Lost in his thoughts, Mick didn't notice the man who sidled up next to him until he heard, "Young fella, how're you doing?"

Mick sized up the old man, wondering if he was friend or foe.

The stranger removed his hat, revealing a near-balding head that glistened in the sun. "We've howdied, but we ain't shook yet," the fellow said with a smile.

"I beg your pardon?"

"I've seen you about town," the man explained, "and I've heard yer name from plenty of folks, but we ain't been formally introduced." After a short chuckle, he extended his hand. "Jake Langford, local reverend."

This guy sure didn't look—or sound—like any reverend Mick had known. Not that he'd known many.

Langford looked out over the lot with a hint of a smile. "I reckon yer wondering what I'm doin' here."

"I figure I know what you're doing." Mick crossed his arms, ready to do business. "You're here to tell me you'd like to see me out of here, like all the others. And to tell me you'd like to see my place shut down before it even opens."

"Well, if I had my druthers, I'd see 'em all shut down," Langford said. "But that ain't why I'm here. On the contrary. I'm just wonderin' why yer drinkin' downstream from the herd."

"Beg pardon?" For the life of him, Mick couldn't make sense of these Texans.

Langford chuckled. "Seems to me, you'd be drinkin' upstream. Tryin' somethin' different. We've got an overabundance of saloons in town as it is. Why not try yer hand at something more practical? We've a need fer a proper feed store. In fact, this property was going to be used for the new feed store, but Skinner changed his mind. That'd be a good venture, and a profitable one, at that."

"Feed store?" Mick laughed, long and loud. "I don't know the first thing about feed stores—unless the 'feed' happens to be whiskey or gin."

"What about a boardinghouse?" the reverend asked. "Goodness knows we could keep it filled up."

"Don't plan to be keeping any of the fellas through to the morning."

Langford shook his head and looked him square in the eye. "What are you searchin' for, son?" Langford asked.

"Searching for?" Mick wondered if he'd heard right.

"I'd have to say a young fella like yourself must be lookin' fer somethin'. Maybe yer thinkin' you'll find it in this here gamblin' hall you've got yer heart set on buildin'."

"I'm looking to please my investors, Reverend. That's my job."

"A place like this must be very excitin'." Reverend Langford rubbed his chin as he looked out over the property again. "But I have a feelin' a man could walk away feelin' near empty."

"Empty pockets, maybe, but he will have enjoyed himself."

As the older man leaned forward, Mick noticed a jagged scar on his forehead and a dozen questions passed through his mind.

"I understand emptiness," the reverend said. "Been there myself. I could tell you all sorts of stories, if'n you had the time."

Mick looked at his pocket watch, anxious to get back to work. "I'm not sure where this is headed, Reverend."

"You can say what you want about yerself, but that don't change the facts."

"What do you mean?"

"I'm jest sayin', you can put yer boots in the oven,

but that don't make 'em biscuits. Yer no more a gambling-hall owner than I am."

Mick laughed again. "I've been a gambling-hall owner for quite some time now. And I'm not sure what you're trying to accomplish, but if you think you can talk me into changing my mind about The Lucky Penny, you may want to reconsider."

The man's expression remained the same. "No man can change the mind of another. But if you'll give me a minute or two, I'll be happy to explain where I'm headed with all this."

Mick gave a curt response. "Talk fast. I'm a busy man."

The reverend's brow wrinkled. "When I was a young feller in Albuquerque, not much more'n a boy, I had an eye for nice things. No money to buy 'em, so I got in the habit of stealin'. Started small. Candy from the mercantile, that sort of thing. Then one thing led to another and before you knew it, I was takin' from folks in a big way—robbin' at gunpoint, even." He shook his head. "Hard to imagine now, ain't it?"

"Well, I certainly never met a preacher who'd spent the better part of his life running from the law, if that's what you mean." A chuckle escaped from Mick's mouth.

"I didn't run fer long. The law caught up with me in Denver. I'd robbed a man who happened to be armed. He shot me three times. Hit me in the belly. I spent several days in the jailhouse with the doctor tending to my wounds. Many was the time I thought I was a goner. But God—"

"God met you in the jailhouse?"

"I guess you could say that." Reverend Langford smiled. "Truth is, He sent a pretty young thing to carry in my meals. She had such a peaceful way about her, always whistling and singing about the love of the Lord. I'll admit, it was her beauty that caught my eye at first. But sooner or later, those stories she told me were naggin' at my conscience."

"What stories?"

"About a God who could forgive, and give me a second chance—if I was willin' to change, to give my heart to Him. She told me that He would forgive me my past, and give me a fresh start. And that's just what happened."

"I see," Mick said politely.

The reverend gave him a pensive look. "God'll do the same for you, if you ask."

Didn't sound quite like Mick would expect a sermon to sound, no hellfire or brimstone at all. Surely Ida had outdone the reverend in that respect. The man's words were kind but firm. Still, the effect was the same as if he'd heard them hollered down from a pulpit with a finger pointed directly at him.

"Thank you, Reverend Langford, but God and I parted ways a long time ago, and I don't think we have much to say to each other these days. However, I do appreciate your stopping by." Mick shook the man's hand and then saw him off the property.

Mick left the site that evening with a headache, more exhausted than he'd been in months. The sun had barely tucked itself in for the night when Mick decided to turn in. Unfortunately, he couldn't sleep. He tossed and turned, thinking about the reverend's words. For whatever reason, he couldn't seem to shake them.

Whether Mick wanted to admit it or not, the fellow was right on some level. He did feel empty. And alone. Odd, how you could feel that way in the midst of so many people. What was it the old guy had said again? *You can put your boots in the oven, but that don't make 'em biscuits...*

Despite that riddle rattling around in his head, Mick was finally able to drift off to sleep.

## Chapter Twelve

On Wednesday afternoon, Ida was pondering the gambling-hall situation in a less volatile state of mind. After several days of thinking through Reverend Langford's Sunday sermon on forgiveness, she decided she'd best keep her temper in check, lest it get the better of her and spoil her whole plan.

It had taken several days, but Ida had indeed come up with a plan. She would arrange a protest, with the help of others in the community, of course. Surely if they linked arms, God would move on their behalf. The shopkeepers would join her, no doubt. A petition was in order, and maybe even a march through the center of town, ending at Mick's site. And if she was very lucky, she might even be able to convince her father's men to stop working for him.

Yes indeed. Together they would end Mick Bradley's dream of building a gambling hall in the town of Spring Creek.

In this excited frame of mind, Ida stopped at the

church to speak with Reverend Langford on her way into town. She wanted to ask him if she might use the church for a planning meeting. He met her on the front steps of the tiny building with a smile.

"Howdy, Ida. Pleasure to see you. What brings you here midday?"

She mustered up the courage to speak her mind. "Reverend, I've come to ask a favor."

"What can I do fer ya?"

"I know we have spoken in the past about Mr. Bradley and his gambling hall."

"Sure, sure. And I need to update you. I talked to Mick yesterday afternoon. Seems like a right nice fellow, though a bit off course," the reverend said.

Perhaps this would be harder than she'd thought. If Mick Bradley had won over the reverend with his persuasive speech, Ida had a tough road ahead of her. "Yes, he is a nice man, I'm sure," she responded. "But that doesn't change the facts. His plan to build a gambling hall puts our town—and its residents— at greater risk than ever. With that in mind, I would like to ask your permission to hold a meeting at the church this evening after midweek service to discuss a plan of action."

The reverend gave her a pensive look. "Instead of talkin' about him, why don't you invite him to join us at the meetin'? We'll see if we can't reason things out with him—let the love of Christ shine through. Wouldn't that be the best way to handle things?"

"I just can't help thinking it's a bad idea to involve

him without talking things over with church folks first, to get their input. Surely, if we all put our heads together we can come up with a practical solution to this problem—one we can all live with, including Mr. Bradley."

The reverend let his hand rest on her arm. "We must be careful in our approach, Ida. We don't want to get folks riled up. Goodness only knows what they'll do if they get too upset."

"Oh, no. Indeed. I'm looking for a peaceful resolution to this problem, I assure you. Perhaps start a petition, that sort of thing. Maybe hold a prayer meeting in front of Mr. Bradley's lot. I want to see this come to a satisfactory conclusion—for everyone."

"Truly? For everyone?"

She swallowed hard before answering. "Truly, Reverend. I want the best for Mr. Bradley, whether it appears that way or not. I'll admit I haven't exactly shown him the kindness of the Lord. I let my temper get the best of me, and spouted off like a teakettle gone to boil. But I've prayed about that and asked God to forgive me."

"Have you, now?"

"I have. I don't mind admitting that I still have my doubts about whether he'll come around. But I think we stand a far better chance of convincing him if we band together." After a brief pause, she added the words that had been nagging at her conscience all along. "I want him to be won to the Lord. Truly I do. I can think of no happier ending."

"Mmm-hmm."

"Mr. Bradley just needs a bit of convincing, is all." Ida's excitement grew as she spoke. "We'll show him the light—one way or another. And I promise to pray before the meeting. In fact, I've been praying ever since the man came to town." Indeed, she wasn't sure when she'd ever spent so many hours in worship.

"Well, I will add my prayers to yours, then, and we will see what the Lord does." Reverend Langford offered up a comforting smile. "In the meantime, feel free to use the church for your meeting tomorrow night. But promise me you will talk with your father about this first. I don't want to come between a man and his daughter."

"Thank you, Reverend, I will."

Ida fanned herself as she continued on into town. One meeting with the fine church folks of Spring Creek should suffice. She would present her case, focusing on the safety and well-being of the children. She would remind folks how simple—how safe— their lives were before the saloons came in.

Then, when she had them convinced, Ida would turn her attention to a reasonable plan of action. They would pray, of course. And with everyone in accord, they would pay Mick Bradley a visit at his construction site for a peaceable demonstration—one meant to make their position quite clear. Surely he could be persuaded to listen to a group of folks who approached him in Christian love.

Ida pushed aside images of Mick's handsome face

and tried to stay focused on the task at hand. *We're not trying to drive him out of town…necessarily.* No, she would be more than happy to see him stay—once he saw the error of his ways.

Mick watched as the exterior walls of The Lucky Penny started to go up. He could see it all now—this building would be a gem, standing out above every other place in town. It would be an establishment local folks could brag about, and one that would draw railroad men from near and far, bringing revenue into Spring Creek in a number of ways.

Yes, the locals would no doubt eventually link arms with him and offer their support once they realized he wasn't here to hurt them. Of course, he hoped to make a profit from the gambling hall. So did his investors. But their success would mean success for the townspeople, as well.

As Mick pondered these things, Ida Mueller hurried by. Mick gave her a nod, and added, "You're late."

She paused and looked up at him. "Beg your pardon?"

"You always arrive a few minutes after two." He reached for his pocket watch and gave it a glance. "It's nearly two-thirty. You're late. Later than usual, I mean."

"Well, I've had other business to attend to this afternoon. Let's just leave it at that," Ida said.

"I do hope the railroad men haven't been a bother."

"Not this time." Ida's brow furrowed as she looked

at the construction going on. "I see you've been busy." Her words sounded strained.

"Yes. Things are going well. Listen, Miss Mueller, I don't want to be at odds with you. Can't we come to some sort of arrangement where we agree to disagree? That sort of thing?"

She used the back of her hand to tuck a loose hair behind her ear. "Mr. Bradley, while I applaud your entrepreneurial efforts, I cannot—and will not—support the gambling industry or another place of business that provides alcohol to the men." Her hands began to tremble, and he watched as she pressed them behind her back. "As long as you insist upon proceeding with your current plans, any hope of finding common ground is out of the question."

"So there's nothing I can do."

"There's plenty you can do," Ida responded passionately. "I'm going to ask you one more time to reconsider. Use this piece of property for something other than what you've planned. Please think of the families, the children."

The pinging sound of hammers against nails continued. Mick looked at the building—could almost see it in its full glory now. He turned back to her.

"I'm sorry," he said. "I'm a businessman, Miss Mueller, and it's my job to build this hall."

She let out a lengthy sigh and turned to enter the mercantile, her skirts nearly getting tangled around her feet.

Mick watched her go, saddened that he was on

the opposite side of the fence from the one person whose opinion suddenly meant more to him than almost any other.

Probably best if he didn't think about the implications of that.

## Chapter Thirteen

The Wednesday-evening church service drew to a close and Ida shifted in her seat, anxious for the meeting to begin. She looked at her papa for reassurance. They'd spent their dinner hour talking through a plan of action, during which he had done his best to convince her that more flies could be caught with honey than vinegar.

Ida wasn't completely convinced. Continuing to pray for Mick would be the best plan of action, according to Papa. That, and encouraging others to pray for him, as well. Then, if the church folks agreed, they would hold a prayer meeting in town in front of the gambling-hall site, followed by a meeting with Mr. Bradley to discuss other options for his new building. Perhaps the walls of Jericho would come tumbling down if the good Christian people of Spring Creek would unite and pray.

And perhaps, in taking a slightly softer approach, the Lord would somehow reach Mick, cause him to see things in a new light. Papa seemed convinced, and Ida dared hope—in spite of his words earlier this afternoon—that Mick Bradley might be persuaded to reconsider his current plans.

As the service ended, Reverend Langford addressed the congregation. "We'll be takin' a break for about five minutes, then I'll be callin' the meetin' to order."

The congregants stood and stretched their legs. Several of the womenfolk approached Ida to thank her for taking such a strong interest in the town.

Mrs. Oberwetter, a widow, said, "You're a brave girl to take on a goliath like Mick Bradley."

"I hear you're the one behind this meeting, Ida," Mrs. Gertsch offered as her eyes filled with tears. "I believe your mother would be so proud of you. She was a woman of strength, and you're so much like her."

"I…I am?"

"Oh, indeed." The older woman slipped an arm around her shoulder. "She was always one to protect others. I see you've inherited that same spirit." She leaned in close to whisper in her ear. "Just let the Lord lead you, child. Don't get ahead of Him."

"I won't." *I hope.*

Reverend Langford called the meeting to order, than prayed a heartfelt prayer for Mick Bradley. As Ida listened to his words, her heart seemed to flip-flop. Though she wanted to see an end to Mr. Bradley's gambling hall, there was still something about the man that very nearly caused her to lose control of her senses. It was such a confusing sensation, given that he stood for everything she felt was wrong with Spring Creek.

After praying, the reverend turned the meeting over to Ida, who approached the front of the room with her knees knocking. She wondered if this was how Esther had felt. Did her throat feel tight and constricted? Did her hands shake? Did her feet feel like mush?

As Ida turned to face the crowd, she took a moment to look at the faces of all in attendance. She'd known and loved so many of these folks since birth. Many of the women had swept in when her mother died, looking after her as best they could.

She would do no less for Spring Creek's children. She would follow in her mother's footsteps, caring for those who could not care for themselves.

With courage mounting, she began to speak. "I want to thank you all for staying for the meeting, and special thanks to Reverend Langford for allowing me the privilege of speaking out in the church. I count it an honor.

"As you all know, we're here to discuss the building of the new gambling hall. Now, I know as individuals we've spent many an hour in prayer about this already, but I also know there is power in the prayer of agreement. That's why I've asked for a bit of your time this evening. I've heard some of the scuttlebutt about Mr. Bradley's gambling hall. I've even been a part of it, I must confess. But merely talking about it isn't the right approach. I believe the Lord is calling us to do more."

Ida's thoughts shifted at once to Esther. Her heart stilled a bit and she forged ahead. "We can talk all day and night, but folks are still going to come into our town and build what they like. Truly, the only resolution to this is prayer, followed by carefully thought-out action."

The crowd began to stir, and she stilled them by raising her hand. "Surely the Lord would have us link hands and hearts in prayer and in action. I would like to suggest a civilized meeting with Mr. Bradley on his lot, but not until Saturday. We need time to pray first—to seek the Lord for what He would have us say. When we are all in agreement, we will choose one of the men to represent us as we all stand face-to-face with Mr. Bradley."

She paused a moment as she contemplated the image of the congregation standing in front of Mick Bradley. How would he respond? Could he be persuaded?

"This is my suggestion, anyway," she continued. "With that in mind, perhaps some of you have questions or suggestions."

Hands quickly went up all over the place. Mrs. Gertsch quoted a lengthy passage from the Bible, advocating a prayerful approach. Mrs. Oberwetter interjected, suggesting they run the man out of town on a rail before Spring Creek's children were swept away by the raging tide of sin and corruption. Papa countered with a passage on love, and several of the other men offered their middle-ground thoughts.

"I don't believe it's necessary to insist upon Mr. Bradley's leaving town," Ida explained. "Though I felt so at one time. Papa has convinced me—and Reverend Langford, too—that the Lord must've had a reason for bringing Mick Bradley to Spring Creek. And surely we—" she gestured around the room with a smile "—are part of that reason. Now let's get to work and see if we can win Mick Bradley to the Lord."

No sooner were the words spoken than the back door to the church opened. Ida gasped aloud as Chuck Brewster and the other saloon owners entered. Brewster removed his hat and nodded in her direction, then took a seat in the back pew, the others joining him. Folks turned around and stared.

The reverend went back to welcome the men. As Ida watched him shake hands with Chuck Brewster, a shiver ran down her spine. She couldn't help but think that these rough and rowdy fellows had a plan all their own.

Late Wednesday evening Mick finished up his dinner at The Harvey House and took a stroll down Midway, curious as to why the street seemed so deserted at eight o'clock in the evening. He noticed a bit of activity coming from Brewster's place, but other than that, very few people came and went—a fact that confused him.

"Ah, yes," he said aloud as he remembered. Wednesday night. The townsfolk were likely in church.

The strangest sensation came over him as he

thought about Reverend Langford. Was he standing up in front of the congregation now, preaching? Convincing folks of the error of their ways? Was Ida sitting in the front pew, hanging on every word? Preparing another speech about the sinfulness of his plans?

Mick turned his attention back to the nearly empty street, noticing a couple of men ambling in his direction, likely fresh off the evening train. As he approached the mercantile, he saw an unfamiliar man with dark hair, a bit younger than himself.

"Mercantile closed?" the fellow asked.

"Yes, they close at five," Mick said. "Half the town's in church tonight, anyway."

"I wondered why it was so quiet around here." The man stuck out his hand. "Johnsey Fischer. Just got off the train. I work for the Great Northern."

"Mick Bradley," Mick said, nodding his head. "You staying in town?"

"Harvey House," Johnsey replied. "Seller's is full up. And I don't think it'd be wise to rent a room at Wunsche Brothers. Too much going on over there." His cheeks turned red, and Mick nodded in understanding. So this was a good boy. Well, no problem there. Despite what Ida seemed to think, Mick didn't care much for the houses of ill repute—he'd rather men spend their hard-earned money on liquor and cards, not women.

Johnsey tipped his hat and turned back toward the hotel. Mick continued on with his walk, and then returned to his room to get ready for bed.

Just as he was falling asleep, Mick awoke to a suspicious sound outside his door. He rose from the bed and inched his way across the room, then leaned his ear against the heavy wood to listen. A rustling of paper and rapid footsteps moving away piqued his curiosity. Looking down, he noticed a piece of paper on the floor. He picked it up, startled to find the words, "Stay in Spring Creek at your own risk."

The note must've come from Brewster or one of the other saloon owners. Would they act on this threat, or was this some sort of a bluff? He read the words over several times. Surely they were meant to inflict fear, though anger rose in him instead of intimidation. He'd faced tougher adversaries in the past. These Texans wouldn't get to him.

Mick decided he'd better check on the lot. He dressed quickly, grabbed a lantern and made his way over. A scrap of paper had been tacked to the front exterior wall, one that left nothing to the imagination. "The train north leaves at three. Be on it."

Mick turned on his heel. He knew, of course, that Chuck Brewster would be standing outside The Golden Spike with a cigar dangling from his lips, looking his way.

What he didn't know was that half a dozen of Brewster's henchmen would be standing alongside him.

## Chapter Fourteen

Ida rounded the corner onto Midway at the usual time, surprised by the crowd in front of Mick Bradley's lot. The sheriff stood near Mick with his arms folded at his chest, and a concerned look on his face. The workmen appeared to be closing up shop for the day. Strange, at two in the afternoon.

And Mick. She couldn't help but wonder at the look of pain in his eyes.

Ida groaned internally as she saw that the exterior of the structure had gone up. It was a fine-looking building, as buildings went. If only he could be persuaded to reconsider its purpose. On the other hand, it looked as if Mr. Bradley had a lot to contend with this fine day.

Ida hoped to overhear a bit of the conversation but the sheriff turned and walked away just as she passed by. Was it possible their prayers had already been answered? Surely something had happened here.

Ida entered the mercantile and looked around in

amazement at the crowd. The stirrings next door had certainly increased their business.

As she untied the ribbons on her bonnet, Ida tried to catch Dinah's eye. Her aunt tended to a customer at the register, too focused on her work to respond to Ida's inquisitive look. A short time later the crowd thinned and Ida finally had an opportunity to ask, "What has happened next door, Dinah?"

Her aunt spoke in a lowered voice. "Some of the men threatened Mr. Bradley last night. I heard the shots fired myself. It was terrifying."

A shiver ran down Ida's spine, and she found herself wondering if Mrs. Oberwetter's approach might not be best after all. Driving the saloon owners out of town—Mick Bradley included—would put a stop to all this nonsense once and for all.

Dinah let out a sigh, the crease in her brow deepening. "I prayed that the saloon owners would link arms with the church folks and approach Mr. Bradley in a peaceable way. It is certainly not God's plan to drive the man out of town with threats and physical violence." Her aunt shook her head. "I have the strangest feeling, Ida."

"What do you mean?"

"Perhaps he's not the villain we've made him out to be."

"You can say this when your life was in danger because of him last night?"

"Ida, it wasn't Mr. Bradley organizing mobs and brandishing firearms. And the sheriff wouldn't even listen to his story until this afternoon. He's not being treated fairly. Maybe he is just a man—"

"Set on bringing more grief?" Ida crossed her arms. "I will continue to pray. I know you will, too. But this situation seems to be getting worse every day, not better."

She quieted her voice as an unfamiliar customer approached. The man looked to be in his early thirties, with dark curls and a well-trimmed mustache.

"Can I help you?"

Ida noticed that Dinah's cheeks flushed as she spoke.

"Yes." The fellow nodded. "I wonder if you might help me locate the home of a—" he glanced down at a piece of paper in his hand "—Mrs. Gertsch."

"Emma Gertsch?" Dinah asked.

He gave the paper another look. "I suppose. They didn't give me a first name."

"May I ask who 'they' is?" Ida said.

"The folks at The Harvey House," he explained. "That's where I've been staying. But to be honest," he said, lowering his voice and looking around before continuing, "it's too rowdy in town. With all the noise and fighting, I think I'd prefer something a little farther out. I understand there's a Mrs. Gertsch who has rooms to let."

"She does, although I can't be sure of her situation at this time," Dinah said. "She lives just up the road apiece. I would be happy to give you directions."

The fellow flashed a contagious smile. "I'd be in your debt, Miss…"

"Hirsch. Dinah Hirsch."

"Nice to meet you, Miss Hirsch." He folded the paper and put it in his pocket. "Johnsey Fischer from Centerville. I work for the Great Northern," he said, extending his hand.

"N-nice to meet you." Dinah's gaze shifted to the front door as the bell jangled. She quickly withdrew her hand as another customer entered the store.

"I have such fond memories of this place after my last visit," Johnsey said. "But Spring Creek has changed since I was here last."

Ida wondered if they had discovered a kindred spirit here, someone who might be able to help them save the town. "How long has it been?"

"Three years." He shook his head, a forlorn look in his eyes. "And true, the place has grown. But I'm referring to more than just a physical change. Something I can't quite put my finger on."

"You needn't say more." Dinah sighed. "I see the transformation all too clearly, and it's not for the better. I pray every day the situation will improve."

"Then I will add my prayers to yours." He gave them a sympathetic look.

Carter interrupted their conversation, appearing with marbles in hand. He took one look at Mr. Fischer and promptly began explaining the details of his prized collection. Thankfully, the newcomer appeared to be taken with the child and spent several minutes talking with him.

The fellow finally left, and the color seemed to go

out of Dinah's cheeks as he did. Ida took note but did not say a word. Instead, she went on about her business, tending to the needs of shoppers, including Myrtle Mae.

"I heard about what happened next door," the older woman whispered. "And I'm praying for you all, honey. For your protection."

As Myrtle Mae left, Chuck Brewster came in. As was often the case, he was seeking chewing tobacco and coffee, along with crackers and peanuts. He gave Ida a curt nod after she waited on him, and she returned the gesture out of politeness, though a chill went through her. Had this man been responsible for the shots fired at Mick Bradley? If so, had something in their meeting last night stirred him to action?

Ida took a peek out the window and saw Mick standing in front of his new building. A feeling of shame swept over her. Perhaps she'd been too hasty in condemning him. Maybe, with a bit of help from above, he might see the error of his ways—if she left the matter in God's hands and didn't try to handle this on her own.

Another glance out the window at Mick's stooped shoulders and somber expression convinced her once and for all to release both her bitterness and her determination to fix this situation—and to do exactly what she'd told the church folks she would do. Pray.

Perhaps in her haste to become like Esther, she

had overstepped her bounds. Surely the time had come to step aside, and just let God…be God.

Mick Bradley had never been one to tuck his tail between his legs and back his way out of town, even in the worst of situations. Still, as this nuisance of a day continued, the temptation to do just that gradually took hold.

A man should be safe, standing on his own plot of land, shouldn't he? He shouldn't have to duck passing bullets, or fend off foul-mouthed ruffians. And yet the last twenty-four hours had brought both, and in just that order.

Last night's bullets, according to the sheriff, must've been an accident—the result of a misfire, perhaps, or a couple of railroad men blowing off some steam. Funny, no railroad men had been nearby at the time. Based on the angle, there was no doubt the shots had been fired from The Golden Spike.

And the drunken visitors who'd paid him a visit moments later, sticks in hand? The ones who'd threatened to take him down if he didn't hightail it out of town? Just railroad fellas, up to no good, according to the sheriff. Mick had to disagree. The threats from Brewster's henchmen had been quite real, and left little to the imagination.

And to top it all off, his workers had abandoned him today. So much for doubling their pay.

Everything about this just had a bad feel to it. Brewster's men would surely continue to harass him, not giving up until he boarded that train headed north.

Maybe he should just save them all the time and trouble and do just that.

## Chapter Fifteen

Ida awoke to the sound of shouting and pounding on the door. She followed on Papa's heels down the stairs, fearful of whatever news awaited them.

Carl Walken stood there, gasping for breath, with a lantern in hand. Even with only the tiny flicker of the flame inside, Ida could see that the man was shaking.

"There's trouble in town, Mr. Mueller," Carl said.

"What sort of trouble?" Ida asked.

Carl gestured for them to step out onto the porch. Though the sun had not yet risen, an eerie glow lit the skies, and the smell of smoke filled the air. Ida turned back to her father, eyes wide. "Fire!"

"Where is it?" her father asked, concern etched on his brow.

Carl couldn't respond for a second as he continued to fight for air.

"Mick Bradley's place?" Ida asked.

He nodded. "After all the work we did getting the building up. The whole thing's burned to the ground. Such a waste."

A fierce trembling began in Ida's knees and quickly moved up to consume her whole body. "Th-the mercantile?"

Carl shook his head. "Doesn't look to be much damage there. The west wall is scorched, but I believe it's external only. And I think a couple of windows have blown, but they're easily replaced."

"My sister and nephew?" her father asked.

"They're safe, Mr. Mueller. That's one of the reasons I came by, to let you know so that you wouldn't worry. But we'll know more about the mercantile after the sun rises."

"I cannot wait until the sun rises." Ida turned back toward the door with tears in her eyes. She managed a frantic prayer, thanking the Lord for Dinah and Carter's safety. From the beginning she'd argued that they shouldn't live in town above the store, but Dinah had her heart set on it. If only Papa hadn't sold that lumber to Mick Bradley, none of this would have happened.

Seconds later she chided herself for such thoughts. Her papa was the finest man she'd ever known, and always had the best of intentions. And likely the men who'd set the fire would have never gotten so riled up in the first place if she hadn't created such a stir. Oh, was she to blame for all of this? What if something had happened to Dinah or Carter—or Mick?

She brushed away her tears, suddenly more angry at herself than anyone else.

Papa reached over and patted her arm. "I'll come with you, Ida. We'll take the wagon."

Minutes later, they were making the journey to town. The stench of smoke grew stronger the closer they got. Ida covered her mouth and nose with a handkerchief and tried to hold back the fits of coughing before they erupted. She could scarcely imagine what they might find in town if the smoke was this thick on the outskirts.

As Papa led the team onto Midway, Ida pulled the handkerchief away and gasped. She'd never seen so many people gathered together like this before. Many of the men still wore their nightclothes. Black soot covered the faces and shirts of many of the others.

She looked in the direction of the mercantile. Thankfully, it remained standing, seemingly unharmed, at least from what she could tell from the wagon.

But where were Dinah and Carter?

When the wagon drew to a stop, Ida scrambled down and began to run through the crowd. She couldn't find her aunt anywhere. On she went, through the throng of men, in search of her loved ones. She heard Papa's voice calling out to her but she did not stop.

As she reached the front of the store, another familiar voice rang out above the din. "Ida?"

She looked up to see Mick Bradley. A feeling of

faintness swept over Ida and she grabbed his arm at once to keep from falling.

"Are you all right?" he asked.

She shook her head, and her knees began to go out from under her. She felt herself scooped up and carried down the street, away from the crowd. The coughing fits came in force now, and she took the handkerchief he offered.

Embarrassment washed over Ida in waves, along with nausea and dizziness. She struggled against his arms. If only he would put her down, she could find her aunt and cousin.

"Please…please put me down," she managed at last.

"Are you sure?"

When she nodded, he eased her down, though he didn't release his grip around her waist.

"I'm fine. I promise." She waited a moment for the dizziness to pass. "Do you know where Dinah and Carter are?"

"They've been taken nearby to The Harvey House," he explained. "I was taking you in that direction so you could be together."

"I think I can make it the rest of the way on my own." She squinted to see through the thick cloud of smoke.

"I'd feel better if you let me escort you there myself," he said. "Please." He sounded like a completely different man than the one who'd offered to walk her into town all those days ago. How could she turn him down?

She nodded and he extended his arm. She took it,

if for no other reason than to keep her knees from buckling. Within minutes, they were climbing the stairs to the hotel. He pulled open the door, and right away she saw Dinah and Carter seated in the lobby on the velvet sofa, still dressed in their nightclothes. Carter clutched the puppy in his arms. To Ida's great surprise, Nellie DeVries sat nearby tending to her aunt and cousin. So did Johnsey Fischer. Ida couldn't help but notice the look of concern in his eyes as he cared for Dinah.

"Dinah!" She ran to her aunt, arms extended. "I was so scared." After a lengthy embrace, she grabbed Carter, wrapping him tightly in her arms. "I don't know what I would have done if something had happened to you—either of you."

Carter's eyes grew wide. "I saw the flames, Ida! They were taller than the store—all the way to the sky."

"You're my big, brave boy." She placed several kisses on his forehead in haste. "I am so glad you are unharmed."

Just then the hotel manager appeared with a sheet in hand. Dinah wrapped it around herself to cover her dressing gown. "I wish I could say the same for the store," she said with a groan.

"What happened to it?"

"The windows on the west wall were shattered during the explosion, and the outside wall is scorched, I'm sure."

"Explosion?"

"Oh my, yes." Dinah shook her head. "This started

with the most awful explosion. And the flames were so close." Her hands began to tremble. "It was terrifying."

"I can't even imagine."

"I heard it myself," Nellie said. "I was in a sound sleep, but the noise woke me up. Took me a minute to figure out where it had come from, but I went running into the mercantile the minute I saw the flames."

"You…you saved Dinah and Carter?" Ida asked, amazed.

"Well, I would hardly say that." Nellie's cheeks flushed. "They were already headed down the stairs. I just offered a bit of assistance to get them out the door."

"She helped me with Carter," Dinah said. "And she went to fetch the puppy from out back. Truly, I don't know what I would have done without her. I could scarcely collect my thoughts, I was so afraid. You know how it is when you're awakened by something frightening—you can hardly think straight."

"Yes, I know," Ida agreed.

Dinah shook her head. "The smell of smoke is bound to have settled into everything porous. There's no telling how many things in the store will have to be disposed of. The bolts of fabric, for instance. And anything else that might have absorbed the odor." She shook her head and tears followed. "And we have a lot of water damage, as well."

"Dinah, I'm so sorry." Ida knelt down at her aunt's side and took her hand. "But Papa and I are here now, and as soon as the sun is up, we will start working. I'm sure others will help."

Mick, quiet till now, said, "I'll see if I can gather my workers, and they will be at your disposal. Anything you need…"

With a tip of his hat, he excused himself to tend to that task.

"And I'll talk to some of the girls," Nellie offered. She bounded from her spot next to Dinah, sprinting toward the door.

Ida looked at Dinah in amazement. "Who would have thought it?" she whispered. "Mick Bradley and Nellie DeVries coming to our aid. Could such a thing really be happening?"

Dinah nodded and a hint of a smile graced her lips. "I have no doubt they are both troubled souls. But clearly they have good in them, Ida. I truly believe they, like others, can be won to the Lord if we simply live the kind of lives before them that exemplify Christlike behavior."

Johnsey chimed in with a quiet, "Amen."

Ida felt the familiar tug of shame on her heart. "I think, in my haste, I might have judged them too harshly. And not just Mick and Nellie, either. The railroad men, as well. All of them." She shifted her gaze downward as she added, "I never really took the time to get to know them as individuals before drawing such stern conclusions."

No, until this morning they had been sinners, plain and simple. Not even sinners in need of saving. Just sinners in need of, well, a swift kick.

Ida's thoughts shifted to Mick Bradley and she realized that today was the day they were supposed to confront him. *The day we were going to try to reason with him about the gambling hall.*

Now there was no more gambling hall.

She couldn't help but wonder what Mick was thinking right now. If his dream had burned to the ground, would he finally succumb to the pressure and board the train north?

Ida found herself hoping against hope that he wouldn't.

The sun rose, revealing the extent of the damage. Mick stood in the center of the street, looking at what had once been his building. Gone. Not a beam left. Not a stick of wood untouched by the flames. Only the charred slab remained.

He'd awakened to the sound of shouts in the street and had known. In his gut he had known. One glance out the window proved that his plans were indeed going up in smoke.

Strange, the first thing he'd thought about was the folks residing inside the mercantile. As he'd run toward the lot, he had even offered up a prayer, of sorts. If that's what you wanted to call it. Thankfully, he'd seen Dinah and her little boy right away and had offered assistance. Taking Ida to join them had given him a small sense of purpose, at least for the moment, though he had to wonder what she might be thinking about him now. Surely her opinion of him had spiraled down even more, if such a thing were possible.

Now, staring at the damage on the west wall of the mercantile, he couldn't help but feel guilty as he contemplated the truth of it. None of this would have happened if he'd just left town when he was threatened.

But Mick wasn't the sort to turn and run. Never had been, never would be.

Only, where did that leave him now? Likely his investors would not take this news lying down, but neither would they send more money for rebuilding if they heard the particulars. No indeed. They were more likely to insist that he return their money or build elsewhere.

Anger gripped Mick's heart as he surveyed the damage. He should have paid attention to the mood of the town. Many people didn't want this hall. Hadn't Ida said as much? And hadn't others in town been all too clear about their feelings? A sense of failure washed over Mick.

He had no doubt where things stood. A few more minutes of staring at the charred rubble clarified that point in his mind. He would never convince his investors to try again in a town like this. The risk was too great.

Still, as Mick thought about Spring Creek, as he contemplated the fact that the town—or at least one of its residents—had somehow lodged in his heart, he could hardly imagine boarding the train.

He'd just have to figure out another way to satisfy his investors. Because he had no intention of leaving Spring Creek as long as Ida was still here.

# Chapter Sixteen

The next few days were spent working to clean up the mercantile. Ida watched, humbled, as Johnsey, Mick and several of the other local men labored alongside her family members, emptying shelves, washing everything down with soap and water and replacing the missing windows. Nellie stopped by to bring food and water for the workers. Surely Ida had judged them all too harshly, just as she'd told Dinah the morning of the fire.

She prayed about her hasty judgments, asking God to forgive her. Still, in spite of His gentle nudging, she could hardly forgive herself. Many times Mick looked her way with a pained expression in his eyes. She read the guilt there. He felt responsible for the damage to the mercantile; that much was obvious. But would he give up on the gambling hall now, after all that had happened? That decision was in the Lord's hands. No longer would Ida make suggestions, one way or the other.

By Tuesday afternoon all the men had gone back to their regular jobs—all but Mick. Ida secretly wondered why he lingered in the shop, looking for things to do. She watched him out of the corner of her eye as the store finally reopened for business. He seemed to celebrate with the others, smiling as he welcomed folks at the door.

Ida pushed a few loose hairs out of her face and surveyed the store with a keen eye. Yes, it would be some time before new bolts of fabric arrived, and certainly the smell of smoke lingered in the air, but folks still came, as always. In fact, some arrived in haste, anxious to make their purchases.

"Glad to see you back up and running," Orin Lemm said, as he purchased razor straps.

Ida thanked him, and sent him on his way with a smile, pleased for the business.

"You've done wonders with the place, Ida," Mrs. Gertsch said with a smile as she traded in her homemade candles for sugar. The older woman then leaned in with a smile and whispered, "I missed coming in to see you."

Ida knew the older woman missed their conversations. And Ida had missed them, too. In fact, she'd missed nearly everything related to the running of the store.

"That Johnsey Fischer is a nice fellow." Mrs. Gertsch gave an admiring smile. "I've enjoyed having him at the house. There's nothing like a man's voice in a place to make it feel like a home."

Just then Johnsey let out a laugh and Dinah, who stood nearby, turned to him with flushed cheeks.

"I've seen that look before," Mrs. Gertsch whispered. "Dinah is smitten."

Ida contemplated Dinah and Johnsey as she turned back to her chores. Her aunt did seem to act a bit strange when Johnsey was around, but they scarcely knew each other. Just a few short days, was all. Why, she and Mick had known each other longer than that and they hardly gazed at each other in such a way.

Ida looked up and met Mick's eyes. Her stomach did a strange little flip and she felt her own cheeks flush with color. Perhaps Dinah wasn't the only one who was smitten after all.

Midafternoon, Sophie and her mother stopped by to drop off a pan of corn bread and a pot of pinto beans.

The influx of townspeople with food in hand reminded her of when Mama had died. So many people had swept in around her, trying to heal her broken heart with potatoes, venison and the like. She hadn't been able to consume much of it back then, but this time around she and Dinah delighted in each new dish.

Ida turned to Mrs. Weimer with a smile. "Thank you so much. You will never know how much this means to us."

"Oh, posh." Sophie's mother gave her hand a squeeze. "Just be sure to share with the menfolk," she said, nodding at Mick. "He looks like he's been working hard."

"And I dare say he's more handsome than ever,

even with his hair all mussed up like that," Sophie said, grinning at Ida. "Wouldn't you agree?"

Ida looked over at him. "He has many admirable qualities." Ida released a lingering sigh. "In spite of my earlier thoughts on the matter."

"Indeed he does," Sophie said, giving Ida a playful wink and heading off in Mick's direction.

Mick turned to face Sophie with a smile, and Ida's heart lurched. As she watched her friend chatting with Mick, a mix of feelings coursed through her, feelings she had not anticipated—and yet could not seem to control.

Mick watched Ida as she closed up shop for the day. She looked tired, he thought. Understandable, given the fact that people had been in and out of the store nonstop, all day long, spending generously. It moved him, to see how everyone in Spring Creek pulled together to lend their support.

Ida glanced his way as he swept the floor. "Are you hungry?"

He grinned at her. "Starved. What've you got in mind?"

"Sophie and her mother brought some corn bread and pinto beans earlier," she said. "Dinah's upstairs warming them up, and she wanted me to extend an invitation to supper."

"Really? You want me to stay?" he asked before he could stop himself.

"I'll admit, it won't be as good as Myrtle Mae's

cooking," Ida confessed, "but it's a free meal, and one you've rightly earned. We'd be happy to have you."

Mick readily agreed and within minutes they were all seated at Dinah's table in the upstairs kitchen, eating mushy beans and chasing down dry corn bread with large glasses of cold milk. As they ate, Dinah and Ida talked through the events of the day, commenting on the various people who'd come in and out of the shop.

Mick found himself thinking about a comment one of Brewster's men had passed his way while in the store this morning. Another threat. *Be on the afternoon train to Centerville or there will be a price to pay.*

It was as if Brewster and his men knew he wanted to stay in Spring Creek. But even he didn't know yet what to do about The Lucky Penny. He had to send word of the fire to his investors, but he couldn't do it until he had a plan.

The women continued to talk, oblivious to his ponderings. Mick finished up his bowl of beans and leaned back in his seat, giving Dinah a smile. "You do quite a healthy business here. And your customers are loyal, to say the least."

"Oh, yes." She nodded. "I've known many of these folks for years. And the locals—the ones who were born and raised here—will do anything to help out when there's a need. It's always been like that."

"Until the last few years," Ida added. "When the Great Northern came through, I honestly thought our little town would never recover from the shock. But it looks like I was wrong, and I'm happy to admit it. It would appear the fine folks of Spring Creek, Texas, still know how to lend a helping hand to a family in need, and for that I'm so grateful."

Dinah whispered a quiet, "Amen," and Mick almost joined her. Right now, seated here with these two women, watching Carter ladle beans from an oversize spoon into his mouth…Mick almost felt right at home.

"It's going to be dark out soon," he said to Ida, nodding toward the window. "I'd be happy to walk you home."

Her face reddened. "Oh, that's not necessary. I'll be fine." She started to push back her chair and he stood to assist her.

"Let me walk you as far as the tracks," Mick suggested. "I'd feel better if I knew you weren't walking through town with the sun going down. It's just too dangerous."

"He's right, Ida," Dinah agreed. "You've stayed much later than usual, and there's no telling what sort of trouble you could run into along the way with the men so riled up. I'd feel so much better if you let Mr. Bradley walk you home."

Ida tried to argue, but Mick—to his great pleasure—managed to stop her before she declined his offer. They said their goodbyes and headed down the stairs and out onto Midway. Mick took note of the fact that Chuck Brewster's men were gathered in a cluster in front of The Golden Spike. He pushed aside the uneasy feeling that took hold, though he couldn't seem to shift his gaze.

The men looked his way as he and Ida turned in the opposite direction. Mick focused his attentions on the beautiful woman to his left, determined to protect her from these ruffians.

They made their way to the edge of town and beyond the tracks. He felt sure she would stop him there, telling him she could make it the rest of the way on her own, but she did not. Instead, they talked easily and at length as the sun settled into a heavy sky off in the west. All too soon they arrived at Ida's house.

"I'm so grateful for your time," Ida said. "Thank you."

"My pleasure." He wanted to say so much more—to tell her how sorry he was that he'd been the cause of so much trouble, to say that he'd figure out a way to make it right. And yet...

As he gazed into Ida Mueller's beautiful eyes, as he studied the color of her hair and the sound of her voice, Mick felt torn between two worlds. Part of him longed to link arms with this Southern beauty, walk her to church and join her as she fought to defend her town. Another part of him wanted to rebuild the gambling hall, give it another go, see if he could make things work—for his sake and the sake of his investors.

Oh, if only he could live in both worlds at once.

"Good night, Mr. Bradley." She opened the front door and took a step inside, then turned back to give him a smile that nearly sent his heart into a tailspin.

With a tip of his hat, he turned back toward town.

As Mick made his way along the road, the vibrant colors of the setting sun faded into a haze of gray. Night began to fall around him, shadows hovering overhead. As he reached the roundhouse, a feeling of unrest came over him.

Something felt…wrong.

Off in the distance, just beyond the building, Mick heard what sounded like hushed voices. Then footsteps. Walking. Then running.

As the sound drew near, he inhaled deeply. He was torn between wanting to run and needing to defend himself. Still, as the darkness swallowed him whole, neither seemed like a viable course.

Mick felt the first hit.

And the second.

By the time the third one came, everything had faded to black.

## Chapter Seventeen

A deafening fog enveloped Mick and he fought to breathe. Every few seconds a searing pain tore across his jaw and his head and the taste of blood on his lips served as a chilling reminder of what had just happened.

He tried to sit up, but the searing pain in his right leg stopped him cold.

*Dear God...*

Mick's thoughts, rapid and scattered, were interrupted by a strange tightness in his chest—a crushing feeling that caused him to wonder if his heart might explode.

He couldn't make a bit of sense out of any of it. Nor could he see. A light, white and hot, blinded him and forced him to think he must surely have drifted into a ghoulish nightmare.

"You all right, mister? Answer me if you're all right."

Mick heard the words but couldn't will his head to nod. Or to move at all, for that matter. Instead, he lay quite still, fighting to remember where he was, what had brought him to this agonizing place. He could taste blood on his lips, and pain tore through his jaw. But it was nothing compared to what he felt in his right leg. He began to lose consciousness.

*"Ready for bed, son?" His mother's voice brought comfort as she brushed the hair from his brow. "Let's say our prayers before we settle in for the night." Her smile, bright and reassuring as always, made him want to bow his knees in prayer. And her beautiful eyes—caring, compassionate. How they danced with joy.*

*He tried to respond, but found himself unable to.*

*"Now I lay me down to sleep... What's next, son? Say the next part."*

*Mick whispered, "I pray the Lord..."*

*She joined him for the rest. "...my soul to keep."*

A gripping pain crushed Mick's chest, as if in an attempt to squeeze the breath out of him, and he could not continue. His arms broke free from their numbed state and he reached up, hoping for some-one—anyone—to ease the pain.

"Mister, don't move. Whatever you do. We'll do our best to help you, but you're going to have to work with us."

*If I should die before I wake...*

Mick faded into a world of dreams.


As Ida took a long, hot bath, she did everything in her power not to think about Mick Bradley. She tried not to reflect on the color of his eyes. She did her best to push aside the gentle sound of his voice as he'd offered to walk her home.

Oh, if only she could banish all thoughts of him. Then life would return to normal. She would get back to work, saving her town from ruin, and he would…

Her stomach knotted as she thought about the possibilities.

He would leave.

The idea of Mick Bradley leaving Spring Creek didn't hold the same appeal it once had. Not in the slightest.

She dressed for bed and prayed before settling in for the night. No sooner had she done so than a knock came at the door. Ida rose at once, knowing somehow that the news would not be good. She waited at the top of the stairs as her father answered the door.

"I-I'm so sorry to bother you, sir," said a breathless Johnsey Fischer.

"Nonsense, son. What's happened?"

"It's…it's Mick Bradley."

A gripping sensation took hold of Ida's heart. "What about him?" She descended the stairs, clutching her dressing robe.

Johnsey stepped into the front hall and she read the concern in his eyes in the flicker of the lamplight. "He's been attacked. At the roundhouse."

"No!" Ida gasped. "How bad is it?"

"It doesn't look good, I'm afraid. One of the railroad men found him. He's barely alive."

"Where is he now?" A violent trembling took hold

of her. Oh, how she wanted to be there. To help in whatever way she could.

"Doc Klein is on his way to the roundhouse as we speak. Dinah feels sure the men will take Mick back to Doc Klein's place within the hour."

Ida wanted to ask a thousand questions. Why the roundhouse? How badly was he hurt? Who did this unspeakable thing?

She knew, of course. Knew that Brewster's men had been behind this. Surely Mick knew it, too. If he was still…

As the word *alive* flitted through her mind, Ida's tears started.

"Dinah wants to be freed up to offer her assistance, if needed. She's hoping you will watch Carter, Ida, if you don't mind," Johnsey continued.

"Of course I don't mind." Ida flew into action, rushing to her room and changing clothes as quickly as she could, a prayer winding its way from her heart to her lips as she raced to and fro.

"Lord, I beg you, please protect Mick. Don't let him die. Oh, God, forgive me for getting the men so stirred up. Lord, I…"

She dissolved into sobs. Mick Bradley was dying…because of her.

Every now and again, Mick shifted into his right mind. He attempted to understand what had happened.

Shouting.

Tugging.

Agony unlike anything he had ever experienced before.

Someone kneeling over him. He heard the tearing of cloth and then felt the person wrapping his leg. But why? As Mick tried to reach down, he found himself restrained and fought against it. He did not want to be led to the bowels of hell bound like a prisoner.

If, in fact, hell was his destination.

Again he fought those who tried to restrain him, but this time their voices attempted to soothe his troubled soul.

"Easy now."

He shook his head, the bitter taste of bile rising up into his mouth. *If I should die…*

Mick groaned in pain as men came from every side—lifting, twisting, pulling…

Through the haze, Mick felt a crowd gathered around, sensed their presence. Surely a band of angels wouldn't have offered any more comfort.

"Let's get him out of here, boys." Within minutes, Mick had been loaded on a wagon and was on his way back to town. Whatever awaited him there was completely beyond his control.

## Chapter Eighteen

Ida paced in the kitchen above the mercantile, trying to remain calm.

"Ida, all the worrying in the world won't make things any better," Dinah said.

"I know, I know." Ida twisted a worn dishcloth in her hands, released it and then twisted it again. Her heart felt much like that rag, as if it had been pummeled and then released, only to take a beating once more. First the fire, and now this.

She turned to face her aunt head-on. "What am I to do? I can't help but worry. This is all my fault. If only I hadn't gotten everyone so worked up when he first came—"

Dinah gripped her hand, prying the dishcloth loose. "The Bible instructs us not to worry, only to pray. And you spoke very plainly to the church folks on Wednesday night, encouraging a prayerful approach to Mr. Bradley. This is not your fault, Ida."

"Still—"

"Whenever worries arise, we need to go to God at once. And I can't think of a better time than now." Dinah took a seat at the breakfast table and motioned for Ida to do the same.

Ida dropped into a seat, her eyes filling with tears. She didn't feel like bowing her head or praying. No, she wanted to join the doctor as he cared for Mick, tending to his wounds. She wanted to jump in and fix things, as always. Only now, she could fix nothing. Perhaps Dinah's idea to simply pray made sense after all.

As if reading her thoughts, her aunt reached across the small table and took hold of Ida's hand once again. This time, she began to pray aloud. "Lord, we ask You to watch over Mick. Bring healing and comfort. Be with Doc Klein as he tends to Mick's wounds. Be with the sheriff as he pursues the men who did this. Make Your presence known in the midst of this tragedy, Father. May every heart turn to You. We place this tragic situation in Your capable hands and acknowledge Your role as Sovereign King and as One who knows all things. Amen."

Ida echoed with a quiet "Amen," then gazed up into Dinah's eyes. "I don't know how you do it."

"Do what?"

"You're so strong, Dinah. You've lost so much, and yet you always manage to find the good in everything. And everyone. You turn to God first, when others would simply panic. And you somehow manage to keep the rest of us calm whenever there's a calamity."

"I struggle more than you know. Especially on

days like today." She brushed away a tear and Ida knew her thoughts had shifted to Larson. Dinah's back stiffened and she dried her eyes. "But every time I reach the point where I feel I cannot go on, I am reminded of the Lord's hand at work in my life. And in Carter's. I must trust Him, Ida. And you must, too."

"Yes. I know."

"He will look after Mick, and will shine His searchlight on those who have committed this awful deed. They will be brought to justice."

"But if Mick should die—"

"Ida, you can't think like that."

"Don't you see, Dinah? Papa's right. I try to fix everything. And everyone. I attempted to fix our little town by making Mick miserable enough to leave. Then, suddenly, I felt as if sending him away was the last thing the Lord wanted. Mick Bradley was sent here for a reason, perhaps to come to know the love of the Lord through our good witness. I see that now. But if he's been killed—"

"We have no way of knowing that," Dinah cautioned, "so don't spend time dwelling on it. We will deal with the details as they are revealed. In the meantime, we must busy ourselves in the best possible way. Doc Klein will likely need my help, as always. He was so kind to train me as an assistant for situations like this. Could I leave Carter here with you so that I might offer my services?"

"Of course." Ida worked to press all fears from her

mind as she stood. "Just promise me you'll send word. If you're able, I mean. And to be careful, Dinah."

"Of course."

Dinah and Ida looked in on Carter as he slept, and then Dinah planted a kiss on her son's forehead. "He's growing up so fast," she whispered.

"Indeed. And he will be such a wonderful man one day, Dinah. I'm sure of it." Even as the words were spoken, Mick Bradley's face flashed before Ida's eyes.

With a heavy heart, she said goodbye to Dinah and settled in to wait for news.

"Son, can you hear me?"

Mick awoke to the sound of a strange voice. Through the fog, he looked up into an unfamiliar face. A man with kind eyes. An angel, perhaps? Had he died?

"Son, I'm Doc Klein." The older man's voice sounded soothing, reassuring. "I'm going to take good care of you."

"What happened?"

"Never you mind that now. Just know that I'm going to do the best I can, and lots of folks are praying for you, so you rest easy."

Mick would have laughed if he'd had the strength. Even if the good folks of Spring Creek banded together to offer up prayers on his behalf, why would the Almighty listen?

A violent shaking began and Mick gave himself over to it. How could he possibly be this cold in the middle of summer? Everything swirled around him in a haze. The taste of blood lingered on his tongue and the pain in his chest grew worse with every breath.

*Dear God, just take me. Please. Put me out of this pain.*

Would death bring an end to the unbearable suffering? Suddenly, he wasn't so sure.

A sound at the door drew his attention. He wanted to turn his head but could not seem to move. He soon heard a familiar voice.

"Mick, it's Dinah. I've come to help Doc Klein as he operates."

"Operates?"

"Yes, son," the doctor said. "We've got some work to do on that leg. And I'll wrap those ribs afterward. See if we can ease your pain."

None of this made any sense. Not a bit.

"I'll be giving you morphine, son," the doctor said, "so you'll be asleep soon. I'll do the best I can to piece you back together."

Mick wondered if he deserved to be pieced back together. Probably not, he concluded. Just as well. The best thing that could happen to him now—and to Spring Creek, and to Ida—was if Doc Klein couldn't put the pieces back together. Save them all a lot of trouble.

# Chapter Nineteen

"I'm sorry, Dinah, but I had to come. Carter is with Mrs. Gertsch. I simply couldn't sit still and do nothing. Not when I feel so…responsible."

For once Dinah did not scold her. Instead, she gave Ida a compassionate look, then brought her in the room to see Mick.

Ida gasped at the sight of him—a bloody, mangled mess. "Oh, Dinah!" She knelt at his bedside, her throat in a knot. She finally managed a whisper. "Will he make it?"

Dinah put her finger to her lips and ushered Ida back out of the room. "He just came out of surgery and Doc says it's too early to tell. He's lost a tremendous amount of blood and has several broken bones. His leg is shattered. Even if he does live…" She stopped speaking and simply shook her head.

"What? Please say it."

"Even if he makes it, he might not walk again. And then there's the issue of all the broken ribs. Doc was afraid his lung was punctured, but praise God, that doesn't appear to be the case. Still, it doesn't look good. But we mustn't let him see that."

"Has he come to yet?"

"No. He's on a heavy dose of morphine and will be out most of the night."

Ida's heart twisted. Dinah reached to slip an arm around her waist.

"We need to be strong for him, Ida," Dinah whispered. "If he sees us falling to pieces, imagine what that will do to him. We have to speak words of hope and give him the best possible care."

Ida nodded and did her best to swallow the lump in her throat. "You are right, of course. And I will do whatever you need me to do."

"Go back to my place and get some sleep. You're going to need your strength over the next few days. I have a feeling we're going to have our hands plenty full trying to care for a patient and run the mercantile."

Ida nodded, though she wanted to stay put and sit at Mick's bedside until he awoke. She went into the room again and gently placed her hand on his shoulder, offering up a silent prayer.

*Lord, I beg You, spare this man's life. Give him another chance, Father.*

*Give me another chance.*

No sooner had she sent the prayer heavenward than Mick's eyes began to open.

"Doc Klein!" she called out. "I think he's waking up."

* * *

*If I should die before I wake…*

Mick fought the blinding pain in his leg and attempted to cry out, but words wouldn't come. He groped about with his right hand, ignoring the throb in his midsection as he aimed for his leg. *Dear God, please let it still be there.* He found the answer to his prayer as his hand lit upon a gaping wound.

He worked to open his eyes. *Have I been drugged?* What in the world had happened to cause such pain?

A familiar face appeared in a haze above him. Ida.

Mick tried to sit up, tried to make sense of things, but his rib cage wouldn't allow it. At that moment, the doctor appeared at his side. "Take it easy, young fellow. You're just waking up from surgery, but you're not well enough to sit up just yet."

"Wh-what—"

"Don't talk. Just lie still. I'm going to give you more morphine to ease the pain. Just let me examine you first."

The man leaned down and touched a stethoscope to Mick's chest.

"You had some major injuries, son," the doctor explained as he pulled away a sheet to reveal a bloody array of bandages. "We operated on you a couple of hours ago. Your lungs are both fine, but you came awfully close to losing your right leg. If not for the grace of God…"

*The grace of God? What kind of a God would allow something like this to happen?*

Mick's head throbbed and he closed his eyes once more. Just as he felt a wave of agony break over him, a small, cool hand grasped his and calmed his racing heart.

"You'll be all right, Mick. You'll be all right," Ida said.

He wished he could open his eyes to see her lovely face, but sleep claimed him once again, the feel of her hand sending him into a deep, dreamless slumber.

# Chapter Twenty

Ida raced through her morning chores at the house and fed her father's work crew their hastily prepared breakfast while still in a groggy state. In the three days since Mick was attacked, she'd had scarcely more than a few moments of sleep, and it was starting to show—both in her actions and in her appearance. But someone had to keep up with the daily routine. And with Dinah so preoccupied now that Mick had been moved to a room above the mercantile, she felt compelled to do all she could.

"These eggs are runny, Ida," one of the lumber-mill workers complained as she slapped them down onto his plate.

"If you want 'em any stiffer, cook 'em yourself."

He shifted his gaze to the plate and took a big bite, not saying another word.

Ida went on dishing out food until all had been served. Perhaps she needed to apologize for her sharp tongue, but with so much festering in her heart and mind she could barely separate one task from another. Exhaustion now gripped Ida, and she struggled not to give herself over to it.

Still, just about every time she started to feel sorry for herself, Ida thought of poor Mick Bradley. She hadn't been able to get him off her mind. His eyes, filled with pain, lingered in her mind, though she tried to force the image away. What was it about the man that captivated her so?

She headed to the kitchen to respond to the whistling teakettle, whispering a prayer for him, asking for the Lord's intervention. Surely Mick needed intervention. He'd hardly spoken a word since Doc Klein operated. She had never seen a man in such a state of brokenness. Daily, she pleaded with the Almighty not only to spare his life, but to touch his hardened heart, as well.

As she started on the dishes, Papa entered the kitchen, interrupting her thoughts. "Daughter, I'd like to speak with you."

Ida looked into her father's soft blue eyes. "About what, Papa?" She reached up with the inside of her elbow to wipe the perspiration from her brow.

He gestured for her to sit, something he rarely did in the middle of her workday.

"If I stop now, I'll never make it to the shop by two o'clock," she said.

"Dinah will do just fine without you for a few minutes, I feel sure."

Ida wiped her hands on a dish towel and approached the table, wondering what her father might want to say.

"There are so many things I love about this town," he began.

"The way it used to be, you mean?" She sat, intrigued by the direction of the conversation.

He shook his head. "No. I mean the way it is now. I love the pine trees, tall and sturdy, and the creek, loaded with catfish. I love the rumble of the trains in the night as they shake the back wall of my bedroom, and the way you can count on them to come and go at just the right time." He smiled. "And I love the way the boys banter back and forth over every little thing."

Ida bit her tongue so as not to speak her mind. He liked the sound of the trains coming and going? How could he? And the bickering of the men? To her way of thinking, the lumber-mill workers took advantage of her father's good nature by conversing too much as they worked.

"You know, Ida," her father continued, "my parents came to Texas because they wanted to be in a place where they would have an opportunity to purchase land at a fair price, raise a family, start a farm. It wasn't until they settled in Spring Creek and saw these beautiful East Texas pine trees that my father considered lumber-mill work. His craftsmanship with pine drew a lot of praise from the locals."

"Really?" Ida marveled at this new insight.

"Your grandfather, God rest his soul, was a man

who genuinely loved people," Papa explained. "And I've always tried to be the same way." He paused and looked at her intently. "It is important to always let the love of God show, even under the hardest of circumstances."

"Of course." She shifted a bit in her chair and wondered at the sudden uneasiness that gripped her heart as he spoke.

Papa's brow wrinkled a bit as he continued. "Just this morning I read one of my favorite scriptures from the book of Timothy. Would you mind if I shared it with you?"

She looked toward the sink full of dishes. "Of course not, Papa."

"Paul wrote this to young Timothy as a reminder," Papa started. "'Christ Jesus came into the world to save sinners; of whom I am chief.'" He gave her an inquisitive stare. "Do you understand why I'm sharing this with you, Ida?" She shook her head.

He reached out to squeeze her hand. "You are, without question, one of the strongest women I have ever known," he said. "But I'm afraid sometimes that your strength works against you." He drew in a deep breath and continued on. "You are so much like your mother, it hurts."

These were new words from her father and they rushed at Ida with a force completely unexpected. "I am?"

"Yes," he responded. "She was always one to fix everything, make everything right again. You have most assuredly inherited that tendency from her. Now me," he said, leaning back in his chair, "I'm more likely to overlook a few of the flaws in a man's life in order to seek out his heart. Give him the benefit of the doubt."

"I've been guilty of judging people harshly, Papa," she admitted. "I know that, and I'm working to change it. Every day I pray about it—now more than ever."

"Of course you do." He continued to hold her hand. "And I'm not saying you're judgmental. More likely, I'd say you so desperately long for all to be well that you feel compelled to make it so."

Tears welled up and she brushed them away.

"I'm not scolding, Ida." Papa patted her hand. "From what Dinah has told me, you have been harder on yourself than I could ever be. I just want to remind you of one little thing. Jesus cannot abide the sin, but He continues to love the sinner."

Ida's gaze shifted to the floor. "I…I know that."

"Of course you do." He slipped an arm around her shoulder. "But we could all use a reminder now and again. That's all." He stood rather abruptly and reached for his hat. "And speaking of loving sinners, I do believe the Lord would have me spend a little time ministering His love to Carl Walken this afternoon. I understand he ran into a bit of trouble in town last night at one of the saloons, and might require a bit of godly counsel."

Her father headed out the back door, all smiles and good nature. Ida went to the sink to finish the dishes, unable to think of anything but her father's words. She was embarrassed that he'd felt the need to speak with her. But he was right, as always.

Love the sinner. It was so simple and yet she'd been so determined to follow in Esther's footsteps that she'd completely lost her way.

It was time to make amends.

# Chapter Twenty-One

As Ida made the walk to the mercantile, no hecklers called out. No jokesters offered marriage proposals. On the contrary, the men in town seemed to avoid her, their eyes shifting away as she walked by. Was it possible that some of these fellows had participated in the attack against Mick Bradley? A shiver ran down her spine at the thought of it.

Ida entered the mercantile, pulled on an apron and took to straightening the shelves. "I have a suspicion you've not rested at all, Dinah. Am I right?" she said by way of greeting.

Dinah sighed, but did not answer.

"Am I right?"

"Nellie DeVries has been by to help on occasion."

Even though Nellie had helped save Dinah and Carter, Ida still could not accept that the young woman carried on every night over at The Golden Spike, doing whatever it was that saloon girls did.

Love the sinner, she reminded herself.

She sighed as conviction settled in. Hadn't she already committed to reserving her harsh judgments? How many catastrophes did she have to go through before she finally caught on? God loved everyone in the town of Spring Creek. Men, women, children—everyone.

And Ida would do her best to love them, too.

Dinah continued. "I tried to prop my feet up for a while around noontime, but with my new boarder to feed…"

"Just as I suspected."

"When I put Carter down for his nap, I struggled with the temptation to join him." Dinah yawned. "But I knew better."

"And now *I* know better." Ida flashed what she hoped would be perceived as a motherly smile. "And I'm telling you to take a nap. You need it, Dinah. You'll not be able to go on if you don't get some rest."

"Oh, I couldn't."

Ida took the broom from her aunt's hands. "You can, and you will. Now don't argue with me. You know how irritable I can be when I'm crossed." She gave a mock scowl and Dinah smiled.

"Yes, I know all too well."

"Then up to bed with you. If your houseguest needs anything, I'll be here."

But before Dinah made it to the staircase, the door opened and Johnsey Fischer came in, hat in hand. Dinah's smile at the sight of him nearly lit up the room.

"How are you today, Dinah?" he asked.

"Fine," she replied.

"She's worn to a frazzle, actually," Ida added. "I'm trying to send her up for a nap."

"If anyone deserves it, Dinah does. I don't know how you keep going, to be quite honest," he said to Dinah, causing her cheeks to redden.

"Have you heard any scuttlebutt about who might've done this? Was it Brewster and his men?" Dinah asked, clearly changing the subject.

"I can't rightly say." Johnsey shrugged. "I'm so new in town that most of these folks are unfamiliar to me, though it makes perfect sense that Brewster would have instigated the attack. Still, everyone's pretty tight-lipped, and I hear the sheriff's having a hard time getting anyone to share any information at all."

"No doubt Brewster's got them all tongue-tied," Ida said. There was a slightly awkward pause as Johnsey looked at Dinah, Dinah looked at the floor and Ida struggled to keep from giggling over what she was witnessing.

Ida cleared her throat as a mischievous idea came into her head. Perhaps she could get some information about Johnsey on behalf of her smitten aunt. Was meddling a sin?

"Until recently, I thought all railroad men were wicked to the core," Ida said with a smile.

Johnsey laughed. "Well, I dare say, many of them are—at least, when they're cooped up between runs. That's when you'll find 'em bored and liquored up.

Rest assured, I'm not like that. And besides, my visit to Spring Creek has nothing to do with the railroad," Johnsey explained.

"Oh?" Dinah said.

"My father currently lives in Centerville, but he recently purchased a farm in the area. It's on the north end of town."

"The Salyer place?"

"Yes, that's it." Johnsey smiled. "My father has always wanted to move back here. And, of course, I plan to live here with him."

Ida noticed Dinah blushing again. How lovely it was to see her aunt like this—enamored, perhaps falling in love. It changed her. She looked like a teenager, full of hope and possibility. Ida hadn't seen her like this in years.

"How wonderful," Dinah said. "Your father will be so happy."

With a hint of a smile in his eyes, he added, "My father will be happy as long as he settles near the creek and can spend his days with a fishing pole in his hand. You should see the look that comes over him when he talks about this place. His memories of Spring Creek are chiseled deep, to be sure."

Ida marveled as she watched the two of them talking. Dinah was getting a second chance and it couldn't happen to a more deserving person. Finally—some joy in the midst of turmoil.

Ida headed to the staircase quietly, not wishing to disturb the small miracle that was taking place in the mercantile.

\* \* \*

"How are you feeling today, Mr. Bradley?"

Mick opened his eyes to see Ida in the doorway. He mumbled a halfhearted response and turned his gaze to the window, not wanting her to see him in such a downhearted state.

"Doc Klein says you're on the mend." Her cheerful demeanor was affected—he could sense it in her voice. Mick knew she blamed herself for his injuries. He'd heard all about the meeting at the church, and how Ida felt she'd riled up Brewster's men.

But he didn't blame her. He had continued building the gambling hall after the trouble started when he should've known better. Now he had absolutely nothing to show for his time here in Spring Creek.

On the other hand, many a townsperson had paid him a visit over the past few days, starting with the good reverend. And Myrtle Mae, with an amazing plate of chicken and dumplings. Her food very nearly rivaled Ida's. He'd certainly been spoiled by these women and their tasty fare.

Maybe these Texans weren't as standoffish, now that he didn't pose a threat. If only his investors would be half as gracious. They'd be looking for their money, plain and simple. And he'd have to figure out a way to get it to them.

"I hate to be a bother," Ida said, "but Doc Klein says I have to tend to your wounds while you're here. I hope you understand." She began to unwrap his dressings.

Mick grunted once again—not an altogether

cooperative patient—and leaned back against the pillows as she went to work pouring alcohol in his wounds until they stung.

"You're not much of a talker these days."

For a second, he contemplated opening up and telling her about his life back in Illinois. Losing his parents at a young age. Getting swept up in the world of heavy-handed gambling-hall owners. Giving in to the temptation to join that world.

Could he tell her about the tightness that took hold of his chest every time he thought about his investors? How they'd come looking for him if he didn't produce enough income to pay then back— and then some—within a few months?

Likely not.

Mick clenched his fists to avoid showing the pain on his face as Ida worked. In such close prox- imity, he could see that her determination matched her beauty. No point in avoiding the fact; the woman was quite lovely to look upon. Hadn't she captured his eye that very first day? Seemed like years ago, not weeks.

Ida explained her actions as she worked on him. "I'm so sorry to have to do this, Mr. Bradley, but we don't want infection to set in."

"I understand. And please call me Mick. If I remember correctly, I asked you to do that some time ago."

She smiled. "And please call me Ida."

Mick nodded, pleased. "I would like the doc to bring me some crutches. I want to get up and start moving. No sense in lying here all day and night."

Ida's eyes widened. "You can't get up on that leg. Not yet. Maybe not…"

She didn't finish. She didn't have to. He understood her well enough, and her words angered him. Deeply.

"Don't talk like that. I'm going to walk again. Doc Klein says I should try to put a little weight on it soon."

"Not this soon. He said in six or eight weeks, and even then you'll have to move slowly."

Mick shook his head in disbelief. This woman was downright impossible at times. "I appreciate the vote of confidence." He regretted the words almost as quickly as they were spoken.

Her eyes filled with tears, and she stood and turned toward the door. "I'm sorry. It's none of my business."

His heart twisted at the pain in her voice. "Ida, please don't go. I'm the one who's sorry. I didn't mean to spout off. I'm just going out of my mind lying here in this bed."

Her face brightened. "We'll get you out of here soon. And if you'd like, I can have your bed moved to the window so you will be able to see outside."

"That would be nice." He looked up into Ida's eyes, taking them in. Her eyes were truly the loveliest things he had ever seen. And that hair, and that smile.

There were worse things than being cared for by such a woman. He should enjoy it while it lasted.

## Chapter Twenty-Two

Ida kept a close eye on Nellie DeVries over the next few days as the young woman came and went from the mercantile.

Nellie had turned out to be a fine helper, and kind-hearted, as well. There was nothing questionable in her demeanor or her attire. She wore a simple calico dress and kept her long, dark curls swept up in a fashionable do. Other than her beauty, there was nothing extraordinary about her. During the daytime hours, anyway.

Perhaps Ida had judged too soon—again. After all, she didn't really know what saloon girls did in the evening. Not really.

"Is there anything else I can do for you before I leave?" Nellie asked late one afternoon.

Ida paused a moment, brushing back her damp hair with the sweep of a hand. "Did you wash out the bandages?"

"I did."

"And you helped Dinah with the laundry?"

"Yes." Nellie nodded. "I've taken everything off the line and folded it. And supper is started, as well." She glanced up at the clock. "If you don't need me for anything else, I really need to get going. It's almost five."

"Of course. Thank you so much for your help."

Ida longed to delve into a very different conversation with Nellie. She wanted to know what happened over there at the saloon and whether Nellie could be persuaded to reconsider the source of her livelihood.

Whatever Nellie did at The Golden Spike remained a mystery, at least to Ida. Perhaps ignorance was bliss, at least in cases like these. Surely, if she knew the particulars, Ida would feel compelled to draw Nellie away from such a place. In short, she would want to fix Nellie. Likely the Lord wanted to take that job on Himself.

Nellie said her goodbyes and headed off. As she reached the door, Sophie entered, nearly running her down.

"Pardon me. Are you all right?"

Nellie laughed. "I'm not one of those china dolls in that case over there. I won't break." She stepped outside and sprinted across the street in the direction of the saloon.

Sophie shook her head as she entered the store. "It's such a shame about that girl. I hate to see her working in a place like that. But what can we do?"

"To quote an old friend of mine, 'This is a matter for prayer.'"

"Indeed," Sophie concurred. "So how's our patient? Is Mick better?"

"I'm very concerned about Mick, Sophie."

"These words can't be coming from the girl who wanted him to leave town so badly." Sophie chuckled. "If memory serves me right, you—"

"Sophie, stop."

"I'm sorry, Ida. I was just teasing."

"Stop. Please. I feel bad enough already."

Sophie gave her a stern gaze. "Ida, you can't do this to yourself. No one bears the blame for what happened except the men who committed the act. And in case you have forgotten, you were *right* to oppose plans for a gambling hall. You're most often right, and I do hope you will keep that in mind."

"Thank you," Ida whispered, attempting a smile. "I can always count on you to cheer me up. You're the dearest person I know."

Indeed. If not for her good friends, Ida didn't know how she would ever forgive herself and begin again.

A man could go crazy lying in bed for days on end. How long could a person lie still? Would he eventually lose his mind?

Lying in bed day after day gave Mick far too much time to think. Thinking was dangerous. Thinking could get a man in trouble, especially when those thoughts were all twisted up around the empty hole in his heart. For whatever reason, he couldn't shake Reverend Langford's story. Perhaps it had something to do with the fact that the man had visited every day since the accident.

And then there were his injuries. The ribs would heal on their own—in time. Doc Klein had done the best job he could to reset Mick's broken leg, but the prognosis was still unclear. With one leg shattered and the other foot sprained, just getting out of the bed proved problematic. If he could get up out of this bed, he would track down Brewster's henchmen and…

And what? They'd already managed to burn down his business and beat him half to death. They'd also managed to elude the sheriff, at least thus far. What other evidence did he need to prove their guilt?

Ida slipped away to the back room, taking a seat atop a closed barrel for a moment's rest after closing up shop. From here, through a tiny window, she could see the burnt piece of land next door and her heart grew heavy. She knew that God had plans for that piece of property, plans that were yet to be evident. Perhaps, after she spent a bit of time in prayer, He would reveal those plans to her.

In the meantime, she had some forgiving to do, and sitting alone gave her the perfect opportunity. Ida poured out her heart to the Almighty, asking Him for the courage to forgive herself not just for treating Mick Bradley in such a manner, but for so quickly judging others, like Nellie.

How long had she been in the business of passing judgment? After a bit of reflection, the truth registered. From the moment the railroad men had laid that first bit of track through her tiny town, she'd become judge and jury. And every step of the way she had used the Bible to spur her on. She'd taken the words of the Great Book and twisted them around to condemn instead of love.

Ida sighed. What a pickle she found herself in. After all, gambling *was* wrong. And dance-hall girls *should* seek more appropriate work. And those whiskey-drinking railroad men *did* need to give up their brawling ways. And yet…

She took a moment to think about Jesus, to ponder the kind of love He had shown tax collectors and prostitutes. He hadn't condemned them, had he? No, surely He had loved them into the kingdom, just as Dinah had suggested.

*Love them into the kingdom.*

Where did one begin after harboring nothing but frustration and animosity? *With prayer. Start with prayer. That is the only place to start.*

With renewed strength, Ida climbed the stairs to the rooms above, determined to show the love of God to all she came in contact with.

She gingerly tapped on Mick's door. As soon as her knuckles rapped against the wood, the trembling began.

"Come in."

She entered with a cheerful smile and he returned it, his eyes lighting up.

"I'd almost given up on you." He gave her a woeful look, one she imagined he'd spent some time rehearsing.

"Nonsense. I'm here every day, as you well know." Ida approached his bedside to check his wounds, doing everything in her power to hide the effect he had on her, but her hands continued to shake. "So, how are you feeling?"

"I'm having a hard time keeping this leg still," he explained. "It seems to have a mind all its own. To be quite frank, I want to get out of bed and run around the room."

"No doubt," Ida said sympathetically.

"I'm not one for lying around," Mick explained. "I'm itching to be doing something. If you can think of anything…"

"Do you enjoy reading? I have quite a few books downstairs." Not that the man would be interested in Mrs. Gertsch's used dime novels, but she felt compelled to offer.

"I suppose I could read a bit. Might help to pass the time. Might even keep me still in this bed without feeling that I'm going crazy."

"There's a Bible on the bedside table." Ida gestured. "Perhaps you could—"

"Maybe. One day."

"Well, staying in bed is best for now. You must let your body mend itself." Ida noticed that his gaze never left her as she unwrapped his bandages. This made her even more nervous. "Looks like Dinah did a fine job of fixing you up this afternoon," she said in an attempt to make small talk. "Clean as a whistle."

"Yes. She's the closest thing to an angel I've seen in a while. So is Nellie. You all are."

"I doubt many would agree with that assessment, at least as far as I'm concerned." Ida couldn't help but sigh. "But I do appreciate your kindness. Just remind me to polish my halo before I leave."

He let out a chuckle then grabbed his midsection. "Oh, don't make me laugh. These ribs of mine are so tender, I can hardly stand it."

"Do I need to wrap you a bit tighter then?" She looked into his eyes and found herself captivated by them in much the same way she'd been captivated the first day they'd met on the street below.

When Mick nodded, Ida reached to help him out of his shirt. She then went about the task of tightening the linen strips around his midsection to hold the ribs firmly in place so they could mend properly. As she worked, she began to feel a bit light-headed. Perhaps it could be blamed on the early-evening heat.

Ida did her best to still the fluttering in her heart and turned her attention to aimless chatter. On and on she went, talking about the weather, the lumber-mill workers—anything and everything to avoid the sudden anxiety that gripped her as she worked to ease Mick's pain. An unusual sensation swept over her, one she did not recognize.

*What in the world is wrong with me?* She rambled on nonstop as she worked, pausing only to look up as a rap on the open door caught her attention. Sophie stood in the doorway.

"I didn't mean to interrupt." Her friend gave her a curious look. "Just wanted to let you know that Dinah needs your assistance in the kitchen."

"I'll be there momentarily." Ida finished wrapping Mick's ribs and helped him back into his shirt. All the while, she felt his gaze on her.

"Is everything all right?" she whispered.

"Mmm-hmm."

As Ida drew close to him one final time to help with his buttons, she very nearly swooned. She quickly stood and said goodbye, scurrying from the room before trembling overtook her entire body.

## Chapter Twenty-Three

Several days went by, and Ida settled into a steady routine. After watching the railroad men in action, she had concluded that they weren't all bad—especially if you factored Johnsey Fischer into the mix. The out-of-towner had become a regular at the mercantile, helping Dinah around the shop, giving up much of his personal time to look after Carter so that she could care for Mick.

Nellie had also wriggled her way into Ida's heart. Still, every afternoon, just before closing up shop for the day, when the young woman excused herself to go to the saloon, Ida felt both troubled and confused. Finally, she could take it no longer. She stopped Nellie at the door.

"If you don't mind my asking, what is it, exactly, that you *do* at the saloon?"

Nellie turned, and with the most innocent face, responded, "Well, I fetch drinks fer the men, mostly." She shrugged. "And I dance with 'em, too. Sometimes I have to pinch my nose to kill off their breath, what with the stench of chewin' tobacco and hard liquor. But I don't really mind. I just do what I can to keep 'em happy. That's what Chuck wants."

Ida felt a wave of nausea wash over her at the mention of Chuck's name. She didn't want to think about him sitting over there at The Golden Spike, going on with life as if nothing had happened. He was responsible for the attack on Mick. Everyone in town knew it. Now, if only the sheriff would find the evidence he needed to arrest the man, all would be well.

"I'm just grateful I don't have to sing, like some of the girls do," Nellie continued. "My mama always said my voice could scare away the chickens. I sure don't want to run off any of the men!"

Ida wondered how she could get Nellie to stop elaborating on her job at the saloon, now that she'd got her started. It didn't seem possible.

"Oh, but I'd really love to be a real showgirl, like the ones out west," Nellie proclaimed. "I've seen some mighty fine ones, especially the gals in Houston, where I worked last." She lifted her right leg, pointed her toe and twirled it around, revealing far too much ankle, and began to sing an unfamiliar little ditty, completely off-key.

"None of that in here now," Ida scolded. She glanced around to make sure no one else had witnessed the girl's sudden display.

"I'll behave—leastways 'round you. I know you don't care for girls like me anyhow. Chuck told me to watch my p's and q's while I was here."

Ida drew in a deep breath, as she tried to figure out a way to explain herself. "It's never the sinner I choose to dislike—only the sin." Almost as soon as the words were spoken, Ida wished she could take them back.

Nellie gave her a pensive look. "Are you sayin' what I do for a livin' is sinful?"

"Well, I can't rightly comment on such things," Ida said. "It's not my place."

Nellie's cheeks flashed pink. "Well, it's a good thing the menfolk don't feel that way. Otherwise I'd be poor as a church mouse." After a brief pause, she added, "I sure wish Mr. Bradley would stay on in Spring Creek and open his new gambling hall."

Ida was so shocked she couldn't respond.

"There's some real money to be made, from what he's been telling me." A smile lit up Nellie's face. "I've been trying my best to convince him to make another go of it. He told me all about how they operate up North, and I think it sounds wonderful."

Ida felt the blood rush to her head. Didn't Nellie realize the danger to Mick if he decided to rebuild the gambling hall now, after everything that had happened? Why, Brewster's men wouldn't rest until he was in his grave.

Nellie leaned in and whispered, "In Chicago, the saloon girls make a commission on all the drinks they sell. The more whiskey they ladle down the men, the more money they make. That sounds like a mighty fine deal to me."

Anger took hold of Ida, but she did not say a word.

"He told me that he'd hire me on the spot, if he ever changed his mind and decided to open The Lucky Penny," Nellie added. "I'd go to work for him in a minute, no doubt about it. Though I don't think Chuck would be very happy."

Ida was more than a little troubled by these revelations. Surely the man couldn't be rethinking his original plan. Hadn't he already laid that idea to rest once and for all?

Nellie took hold of Ida's arm. "I know you don't like what I do, Ida. But my mama's awful sick, and I send nearly every penny I make back to Houston to pay for the doctors and medicine and such. When she's well enough to travel, I want to bring her here to live. That's why it's so important for me to make money. And working in the saloon is the best way for me to do it."

Ida did her best to calm down, though she'd decided to speak her mind to Mick, should he ever again bring up the idea of The Lucky Penny.

"Well, thank you for helping out, Nellie," she said with a nod. "We're very grateful indeed."

"I've enjoyed it so much." In an uncharacteristic gesture, Nellie threw her arms around Ida's neck and gave her a tight squeeze. "And I don't care what Chuck says about you and Dinah. I still feel like we're sisters!"

She turned on her heels and headed for the door, looking back just long enough to wave goodbye. Ida tried to make sense of the conversation they'd just had. Good all mixed up with bad. Nellie saw her as a sister and that made Ida happy. And yet, for all her sisterly qualities, Ida couldn't think of a way to counsel Nellie without the risk of bringing more offense. Perhaps in time the Lord would show her how to approach her new friend with truth. Tempered by love.

Still, all that business about how they did things up North. Ooo! Ida could wring Mick Bradley's neck for bringing up such things in Nellie's company. Did he not realize the temptation his stories presented?

Ida climbed the stairs to check on Mick and give him a telegram that had arrived nearly an hour before. And she hoped against hope that she'd be able to resist that urge to give him a piece of her mind, as well.

A knock at the door interrupted Mick's thoughts. Ida popped her head inside.

"I've got something for you." She stepped into the room. "I very nearly forgot to bring it up. It was delivered more than an hour ago."

"More of Myrtle Mae's pot roast, I hope?" He licked his lips in anticipation.

"No, but an admirable guess."

"Your ham and beans, then? Or maybe that amazing Wiener schnitzel you're so famous for?"

"Not even close." She reached into the pocket of her apron and pulled out a piece of paper.

As he read the words *Western Union*, Mick's heart sank. A telegram. Ida handed it to him and he could see it was from Chicago. He opened it, stunned at what he read. Somehow they knew about the fire, the threats, his injuries—everything. But how? Brewster. Brewster had figured out who'd fronted him the money for the gambling hall and contacted them. Mick would bet money on it.

After a few moments of silence, Ida gave him a concerned look. "Is everything all right?" she asked. "You're as pale as a ghost."

"Mmm-hmm." He folded the paper and stuck it under his pillow. His investors were ending their original agreement and demanding repayment by the end of September. How could he possibly pay them back in such a short time if he couldn't even walk?

"Mick," Ida said, hesitating slightly. "I need to ask you about something. Something that Nellie told me. She made it sound like you're still hoping to open the gambling hall and I—"

Mick held up his hand. "Ida, please. I'd rather not have this conversation. I know exactly how you feel about my plans. But right now, I've got to figure out how I'm going to pay back my investors before they come to Spring Creek looking for me."

"Is that what your telegram was about?"

He nodded, his head aching.

"Well, I'm sorry to hear that, but I don't think the solution is to rebuild the hall. What do you think Brewster's men will do to you next time? They might not leave you alive!" Ida's beautiful cheeks flushed with color.

Mick stared at her for a moment. Slowly, a smile spread across his face.

"What on earth are you grinning about, Mick Bradley?"

"Ida Mueller, I do believe you're worried about me."

Ida opened her mouth to speak, but no words came out. She quickly turned on her heel and left the room before he could say anything else.

"Good evening," he called after her, chuckling.

His laugher was short-lived as the reality of his situation sank in. Even if he started rebuilding the gambling hall now—today—he'd be hard-pressed to raise the necessary funds by summer's end to cover his debt. And Ida was right—once the building started to go back up, Brewster and his men would likely come after him again.

What in the world could he do lying here in bed?

Anger kicked in and Mick fumed over the mess this venture to Texas had become.

Over the next hour or so, Mick watched the sunset through the window. The sky changed from yellow into shimmering shades of orange, and then a fiery, angry red. It seemed to mirror the rage that now filled his heart every time he thought about Chuck Brewster.

Even from the second floor, there was no mistaking the noises coming from The Golden Spike. Strange, when you could hear something but not see it firsthand. He envisioned the dance-hall girls lifting their skirts and exposing slender ankles, drawing the gazes of the men.

All for one purpose, of course. Money. Money spent on drinks, so the fellas could work up the courage to speak to the girls between dances. And money spent on the girls themselves. If Chuck Brewster ran the usual kind of saloon, anyway.

Every now and again, Mick heard the sound of laughter and jealousy gripped his heart. He tried to force it away, but it would not budge. As much as he hated to admit it, Mick envied Brewster tonight. Why should a man like that—ruthless, hardhearted, dangerous—get his piece of the pie and everyone else's, as well?

Mick closed his eyes and images of his gambling hall took over.

He envisioned Nellie at the center of the room, serving drinks.

Heard the laughter of the patrons.

Saw the money changing hands as the railroad men handed over their wages for a bottle of this or a glass of that.

Mick could see it all so clearly. And the more he saw, the more he longed to try—one last time—to make it happen.

# *Chapter Twenty-Four*

Early on Friday afternoon, Ida came up with an idea to lift everyone's spirits, including her own.

"I'd like to have a special dinner tonight with the whole Weimer clan," she explained to Dinah. "I was thinking about doing it here so that Mick could join us."

"A spectacular idea!" Dinah's face lit up at the prospect. "I'm sure your father won't mind having supper in town tonight. And I know how much Mick raves about your cooking. He's probably fit to be tied with my lousy meals."

Ida laughed. "You're a wonderful cook, and your apple strudel is the best in town."

"Then we will have apple strudel for dessert," Dinah said.

"We will give everyone a fabulous meal—one they won't soon forget."

"What's this I hear about a fabulous meal?"

Ida turned to see Johnsey Fischer.

"We are cooking up a feast tonight," Ida said. "Dinah is making the dessert. Would you like to stay for supper?"

"Would I!"

"Wonderful! Dinah, would you mind if I went to Sophie's place to issue the invitation?" Ida asked, pulling off her apron. "I'll be back in just a few minutes."

"Of course. I'll manage without you for a while."

"I'll be here to help her," Johnsey said with a smile.

Ida grinned at Johnsey and practically sprinted out the door. She headed to the Weimer farm just a few blocks from town and found Sophie's mother on the front porch, fanning herself and drinking lemonade.

"Why, Ida, as I live and breathe. You're the last person I expected today." Mrs. Weimer stood and embraced her, then began to fuss with her hair. "I must look a sight, what with this heat and all." She tucked a few loose gray hairs behind her ear.

Sophie appeared on the porch. "Ida! Has something happened? Do you need my help in town?"

"No." Ida laughed. "For once it's good news. I've come to invite your family to dinner tonight. I'll be cooking at Dinah's place. Sausage sauerkraut balls. Dinner will be served promptly at six-thirty. You are all welcome to attend."

"Will Mr. Bradley be sharing the meal with us, by any chance?" Sophie asked.

"He-he will," Ida stammered. It was becoming increasingly clear to Ida that her dear friend had designs on Mick Bradley, and Ida didn't like the way that made her feel. At all.

Sophie gave her a wink. "I still find him the most handsome man in town. What should I wear tonight?"

"Oh, I wouldn't worry about that. It's just friends and family, after all."

As Sophie declared that she would wear her favorite pink dress, Ida's heart plummeted. As much as she hated to admit it, inviting Sophie to dinner might not have been the best course of action. Mick needed to focus on getting well…nothing else.

Unless, of course, that something else had a little something to do with *her*.

Ida quickly chided herself. Did she really want to draw the eye of a man like Mick Bradley, one who clearly didn't yet know the Lord? Definitely not.

"You are so kind to invite us," Sophie said.

Mrs. Weimer's face broadened into a smile. "Yes, thank you for the invitation, Ida. We accept." After a slight chuckle, she added, "With this heat, I wasn't looking forward to cooking, anyway."

"We will see you promptly at six-thirty," Sophie said with a twinkle in her eye.

Oh, if only the invitation could be withdrawn. Then, perhaps, Ida could rid herself of the sinking feeling in the pit of her stomach.

Mick stared at his reflection in the mirror. Not bad for a man who'd spent the better part of the last month in bed. He ran a comb through his hair and contemplated the fact that it needed to be trimmed. Perhaps tomorrow he could call for that younger fellow, Georg, from the barbershop. Right now, he had places to go, people to see—and the idea of getting out of this room lit a fire underneath him.

For once, Mick would share his supper with the others. Dinah had made the suggestion earlier in the day, and he had happily agreed. Though from the smell of things, he would be eating something quite unique, something he wasn't sure he was going to like at all.

Mick reached over to grab hold of the makeshift wooden crutches the doctor had brought by a couple of days ago. Finally! He could get around a bit.

After another glance in the mirror, Mick inched his way toward the door. He'd almost made it when Ida came barreling in, nearly knocking him down.

"Oh, I was coming to fetch you." She gave him a warm smile, though he couldn't help but notice she looked a bit wary. He'd not seen her since their little discussion about his future yesterday.

"I don't need fetching, as you can see for yourself." He took another hobbling step in her direction, trying to stay balanced on the crutches. Turned out it was trickier than it looked. For a second, he very nearly toppled over. She reached out to grab his arm and he steadied immediately.

He felt her hand linger on his arm. They gazed into each other's eyes, and a comforting feeling washed over him. A feeling he could get used to. He refrained from making a comment for fear of embarrassing her and sending her fleeing from the room again.

She pulled her hand away. "The others are waiting in the kitchen."

He made his way along slowly with Ida following behind him. "I've been smelling the food all afternoon," he said, "but I can't place it. What are we eating?"

She laughed. "Likely, it's the sauerkraut you're noticing. It has a smell all its own, to be sure. I've made German sausage sauerkraut balls. They're Papa's favorite. Sophie's, too."

They entered the very full kitchen, and Mick smiled as the others greeted him. Johnsey Fischer had proven to be a likable soul, and Dinah—well, what could be said about a woman who gave her life to help others? Carter bounced up and down in his seat, ready to eat.

Quick introductions were made, though he recognized Sophie's family from that night so long ago at The Harvey House. Funny, he'd spent that evening wondering what it might be like to sit around a dinner table with such a family. Now he would find out firsthand.

No sooner had they taken their places than Ida's father appeared at the door.

"Sorry I'm late." He leaned over and kissed Ida on the head. "Ran into a bit of a problem with a couple of my men."

"It's fine, Papa. We're just glad you're here." Ida gave him a loving smile.

The food was passed, and Mick had just reached for his fork when Mr. Mueller cleared his throat.

"We're going to pray," Ida whispered, reaching for Mick.

Mick allowed her small hand to slip into his own. He remembered her holding his hand once before, when he'd been in so much pain. He'd welcomed the feeling then, and he certainly did now.

They began to pray, and Mick closed his eyes and tried to imagine what it must be like to live like this all the time. How would it feel, to sit around a table every evening with a family of his own?

After the prayer, the noise in the room intensified. Mick bit into one of the sauerkraut balls, more than a little cautious. With relief, he found it to be quite tasty. And so were the accompanying noodles. How could he have doubted Ida? Why, her cooking was by far the best he'd tasted—North or South.

"Do you like it?" she whispered.

He nodded vigorously and took another bite.

A lively conversation ensued, and Mick listened closely, wishing he could join in. Unfortunately, he knew very little about the sugarcane industry, which happened to be the topic at hand. He continued on, eating like a man who might never see food again.

From across the table, Mick caught Carter's eye. The youngster gave him an impish smile, and Mick knew he'd found a friend.

He had to admit—he'd found more than one. Nearly everyone here had proven their friendship to him over the past few weeks.

Especially Ida.

Johnsey piqued Mick's interest when he mentioned the oil strike in Beaumont. "Lots of money to be made in oil," Mick said. "I'd given some thought to moving to Beaumont before I settled on Spring Creek."

"Well, we're glad you chose us instead." Dinah smiled.

"I'm not sure I chose Spring Creek," he replied with a tinge of embarrassment. "It's looking more like Spring Creek chose me."

A resounding laugh went up from everyone at the table.

"It's been that way for many of us," Ida's father admitted. "I dare say most of the residents here had their hearts settled on other places at one time or another. But God seems to draw folks here, like flies to honey."

Mick pondered the man's words. Had God drawn him here? Surely not. The Almighty probably didn't care for gambling halls any more than Ida did.

"Have you given thought to the fact that the Lord has kept you here for a reason?" Dinah asked.

Mick looked across the table, stunned. How could he begin to answer such a ridiculous question?

"I'm not sure I…"

Dinah continued on. "The Lord has spared you and I am convinced it is because He has great plans for you. Texas-size plans."

"For me? I highly doubt that, Dinah."

Johnsey gave him a smile of understanding. "I understand your hesitancy. Been there myself. There was a time when I had made my own plans—laid my own track, if you will. I thought I knew what was best for me."

"What happened?" Mick asked.

"God got hold of me. I was going one way, and the Lord turned me around, sending me off on the track He wanted me on."

"I'm going to be perfectly honest, Johnsey, you don't look like the sort of man who's ever ventured off the straight and narrow."

"Looks can be deceiving, my friend," Johnsey said.

"God has big plans for me, bigger than I've had for myself, is that what you're all saying?"

"Much bigger," Ida said with a nod. "But it means putting your trust in Him."

"Don't know as I've ever figured out how to do that—put my trust in a God I can't see. Whole thing sounds like some kind of a fairy story my mama used to tell me as a child, one I never quite took to."

Thankfully, the conversation shifted as Dinah rose from the table and returned moments later with a plate of beautiful apple strudel in her hand, saying, "I hope everyone saved room for this." She placed it in the center of the table.

Mick sighed as he looked at the tempting dessert. What was it with these people? One minute they were trying to feed his soul; the next, they were heading straight for his belly.

# Chapter Twenty-Five

Ida lay back against the pillows with a pounding heart. She tried to make sense of the feelings that had gripped her since holding Mick Bradley's hand at the dinner table, but could not. Surely the Lord would sweep these feelings away. Perhaps then she could think clearly.

Unable to rest, Ida finally rose from her bed and paced the room. When her heart would not be silenced, she slipped on her wrap and tiptoed out into the hallway. With great care, she eased her way along the wall in the dark, then down the stairs, careful not to wake her father. Opening the front door was trickier, since it tended to squeak. But she made her way out to the front porch without making a sound.

Settling into the porch swing, she breathed in the cool night air. Off in the distance she heard the sound of the train cars locking up. Funny. She'd grown so used to the noise that she scarcely noticed it anymore. It was a comforting sound in a way—familiar.

Ida eased the swing back and forth. The steady movement calmed her, and she closed her eyes.

She had reached for Mick's hand instinctively at the table earlier this evening, never imagining he would take hold of it with such a comforting squeeze. Their hands had fit together perfectly—his soundly grasping hers as if to say, "I am here for you."

Ida opened her eyes, determined to shift her thoughts to something else. She tried to recapture some of the funny stories Sophie had told at the dinner table. But all Ida could remember was the look on her friend's face after Papa's prayer. Jealousy, perhaps? If so, Sophie had no reason to be jealous. None at all.

Or did she?

Mick tossed and turned during his first hour in bed. The elevated temperatures presented a problem, as always, but the type of heat he struggled with tonight had little to do with the weather.

All that talk about God having big plans for him— why did it aggravate him so much? Seemed to Mick his own plans were big enough—building the gambling hall, acquiring the necessary patrons, filling his pockets with cash. Sounded pretty grandiose. Plenty large, even for a state like Texas. Then again, his plans hadn't exactly panned out, had they? And if he didn't come up with the money for the investors by summer's end, he might as well cash it in anyway.

Surely, if the Almighty had big plans for him, as

Ida had suggested, if He *really* wanted him here in Spring Creek, then starting over with the building of The Lucky Penny made perfect sense. Why else would Mick have ended up right back where he started, if not to finish what he'd set out to do in the first place? Strange, he'd never thought about it from that angle before. Someone—or something—wanted him to stay put in Spring Creek.

On the other hand, every time he thought about rebuilding the gambling hall, Mick could picture the look of hurt and disappointment in Ida's eyes. She would not approve—this, he already knew.

He tried to imagine how the conversation would go, what he would say to her, if the opportunity should arise. With a few well-chosen words on his part, she might come around, might see the logic in his plans. She was a reasonable woman, after all.

Mick rolled over onto his side and closed his eyes. He remembered the feel of her hand in his as they had prayed, her soft fingers intertwined with his, and the look of pride in her eyes when he complimented her amazing food.

Whether he wanted to admit it or not, the woman was working her way into his heart.

Mick reached for his crutches and attempted to stand. He wanted to get up and pace the floor but soon realized how impractical that desire was. After a few uncomfortable hobbling steps, he sat back down. As he reached over to light the lantern on the bedside table, his hand brushed up against the Bible—

the same one that had been sitting there for weeks, untouched.

Sure, he'd seen a Bible or two in his life. Who hadn't? But as for really picking one up and reading it, he'd never bothered. Looked like he wasn't going to get any sleep tonight, anyway; what would it hurt to read a few words? He opened the book up and turned to the first page. *Genesis.*

Suddenly, several shots rang out. Mick jolted, and the Bible flew from his hand onto the floor below. A woman's screams filled the night. He struggled to sit up in the bed, the pain in his leg so intense he cried out.

Mick heard footsteps, then a knock on his door, followed by Dinah's familiar voice. "Mr. Bradley?"

She entered the room with a lamp in her hand. Mick struggled to rise with the aid of his crutches.

"No, please stay where you are." Dinah moved toward the window. "I hate to bother you, but I heard shots from across the street. Your window has the best view of the saloon. Did it sound like Nellie's voice to you?" Dinah turned to face him.

Before he could nod, someone pounded on the downstairs door. Dinah disappeared from view and Mick did his best to stand. He wanted to know what had happened. And how he could be of service.

Somehow he managed to make it from the bed to the hallway. He could hear the goings-on downstairs, homing in on the voice of one of the railroad men, asking for Dinah's help. He heard her frantic footsteps as she raced back up the stairs.

She met him, breathless, with the news. "It was Nellie. They're bringing her here because Doc Klein doesn't have room at his place. We'll put her in my room so I'll be close by."

"Of course. What can I do?"

"I'm not sure what we will need. The doctor will tell us. In the meantime, the only thing I can think to ask you to do is pray."

Pray? He hardly knew where to start, but with a nod of his head agreed to somehow try.

Minutes later, a couple of the men eased their way up the stairs with Nellie, pale and limp, in their arms. Blood oozed from her left shoulder, and he tried to assess where she'd been struck. Hopefully not close enough to the neck to be life-threatening. Still, one could never tell with gunshot wounds.

Mick stood in the doorway of Dinah's room as they laid Nellie in the four-poster bed. Every few seconds she would cry out and reach for her shoulder, then she would drift out of consciousness again. Dinah worked feverishly to clean the wound.

Thankfully, Doc Klein arrived in short order, and put Dinah to work boiling water and preparing bandages. Mick sat at the kitchen table, wishing for something, anything to do. He tried to mutter a prayer, but had little to go by. He managed a choppy sentence or two then turned his attentions back to the fellows who'd brought Nellie in. Had these men been the ones who'd caused his injuries? His blood boiled at the very idea. Still, he had to keep his head on straight if he wanted to be any good to Nellie.

The sheriff arrived, full of questions. "Do you know how this happened?" he asked. "Did either of you see anything firsthand?"

"Carl Walken had one too many," one of the fellows said. "Got all riled up about something or another, and pulled his gun on Eugene Weimer."

Weimer? Sophie's older brother?

"I don't think Carl meant to hurt anyone at first," the other man explained. "He got to bragging about something. Started out as a joke, I think. But the next thing I knew, his gun was pointed straight at Eugene, and shots were fired."

The sheriff pulled off his hat and ran his fingers through thinning hair. "Don't look like he's a very good shot."

The man shook his head. "The bullet flew right past him and hit Nellie. She was up on the stage, dancing her heart out."

Mick felt sick as he listened to the story. Sick for Nellie, and sick for Carl and Eugene, who would sober up soon enough and realize the harm their drunken recklessness had caused.

And in the pit of his stomach, Mick also felt sick about the fact that this whole thing could have just as easily happened at The Lucky Penny if he'd carried through with his plans to rebuild.

As the men went their separate ways and the doctor tended to Nellie, Mick finally found the words to offer up that prayer he'd promised Dinah. He said the only thing that seemed to make sense: "God, please help that poor girl." It was his best attempt at reasoning with the Almighty. Surely, with both his leg and his heart in such a torn-up state, the Lord would understand.

## Chapter Twenty-Six

Ida drew near Nellie's bedside with a heavy heart. She knew what Doc Klein had said, of course—that the wounds weren't life-threatening. Still, as she knelt next to Nellie's bed, she prayed for more than just her physical recovery; she prayed for her very soul.

Ida managed to interject a few words on Carl's behalf, as well. And Eugene's. Her mind still reeled at the fact that Eugene Weimer had been in The Golden Spike in the first place. Surely the news must have brought pain to everyone in the Weimer household. Sophie hadn't been by the mercantile this morning, though she usually came to town in the wagon with her mother on Saturday mornings to shop. No, likely today would be spent at home, the whole family coming to terms with what had happened.

Nellie came awake and squinted at the sunlight that peeked in the window.

Ida stood and smoothed back Nellie's hair. "Good morning."

"Ida?" Nellie attempted to sit up, but could not.

"Just rest easy."

Nellie leaned back against the pillows, her face still quite pale from the blood loss. "Wh-what happened?" she whispered. "How did I get here?"

"You don't remember?" When Nellie shook her head, Ida explained. "There was a shooting at the saloon last night, and a stray bullet hit you."

Nellie touched her shoulder and cried out. "Is it bad?" she whispered.

"I truly believe the Lord protected you." Ida took a seat on the edge of the bed and reached for Nellie's hand. "Doc Klein said the bullet came within inches of hitting a major artery in your neck."

Nellie's eyes grew wide.

"The doctor had a doozy of a time getting it out, but you're all patched up now, and he says you should be fine within days. But you have to take it easy. And we have to keep it clean, to guard against infection."

Again, Nellie tried to sit up, a frantic look in her eyes. "I have to get well quick. I need to get back to work. My mama—"

"Don't fret over anything right now," Ida said. "Please. And if your mother needs financial help, I will speak to Reverend Langford. Likely the folks at the church will want to do what they can to assist you."

"Why would the church folks do anything for a girl like me?" Nellie's eyes filled with tears. "Ain't it true what you said before? Don't they think I'm a sinner?"

"I'm sorry I ever said that, Nellie. Sometimes my mouth gets me in trouble. Truth is, the church folks are ready to help anyone in need, whether they know you or not. The purpose of the church is to care for the broken and wounded," Ida explained.

"I do feel broken." Nellie reached for her shoulder once again. "Chuck won't wait long. He'll put another girl in my place. I know he will. So I hope I heal up right quick."

Ida gave Nellie's hand a tender squeeze. "If I had my druthers, I'd keep you from ever going back to work in that saloon. I'd find you a different job, something with less risk involved."

"Oh, but—"

"We will see what the Lord does. In the meantime, you just rest. Please. And let me know when you're hungry. Myrtle Mae came by with some of that famous pot roast of hers."

"Mmm." Nellie nodded. "Maybe after I've napped a while." Her eyes fluttered closed, and Ida turned to leave the room.

As she entered the hallway, she caught a glimpse of Mick Bradley's felt hat on the stand in the corner. Had it really only been last night they'd all shared a meal together? And had he really, as Dinah said, worked through the night to help out?

Surely he must be exhausted today.

Well, she'd have to stop by for a chat to see for herself.

\* \* \*

Mick eased his weight down into a chair at the kitchen table and turned as Ida entered the room.

"There you are." She gave him a broad smile. A good sign. A very good sign.

"Did you need something?"

She pulled up a chair and took a seat across the table from him. "No, not really. I just wanted to thank you for looking after Dinah last night. And Nellie, of course. From what I hear, they both had a rough time of it, and having you here to help meant the world to my aunt."

Mick didn't even try to hide the grin. "You know," he said, "I still can't get used to the fact that she's your aunt. Dinah can't be more than, what…say, seven or eight years older than you?"

Ida nodded. "Yes. My grandmother gave birth to Dinah in her later years. An unexpected blessing— that's what folks around these parts call a late-in-life baby. Papa was an only child until then. My grandmother truly thought she would never be able to have more children." A wistful look came into Ida's eyes.

"Have I brought up a tender subject?" he asked.

"I never knew my grandmother. She passed away giving birth to Dinah. Papa was a grown man by then, and he and Grandpa Max raised the baby by themselves, at least for a time." Looking up at him with a smile, she added, "Can you imagine? Two rough-edged German men raising a little girl? Of course, my papa up and married my mama when Dinah was about five or so, and from what I hear Mama fell in love with her. Took the little tomboy under her wing."

"It's hard to imagine Dinah was ever a tomboy." Mick laughed as he thought about the prim and proper Dinah climbing trees and playing with frogs.

"From what I hear, she was quite a handful. But my mama raised her to be a right fine lady."

"If you don't mind my asking—"

"What happened to Mama?" Ida sighed and sadness registered in her countenance. "She passed away about seven years ago. Yellow fever. Not a day goes by that I don't miss her."

"I'm so sorry. I lost both of my parents some years ago." He reached out and took her hand. Fortunately, she did not pull away. Mick proceeded to tell her his story—how his parents had lost their lives together—and she listened with sympathy. They sat together for a few seconds, hand in hand, until they heard Dinah's footsteps in the stairway. At once, Ida pulled away.

Dinah entered the kitchen, took one look at Ida's flushed cheeks and proceeded to ask if something had happened to Nellie to warrant concern.

"Everything is fine." Ida's gaze shifted out the window. "We were just visiting." She looked at her aunt with a smile. "I was telling Mick what a rough-and-tumble little girl you were."

"You were not."

"I was." Ida grinned and for the first time Mick noticed tiny dimples in her cheeks.

Dinah took to fanning herself as she turned to

Mick. "Well, don't believe everything you hear. Besides, there are any number of stories I could tell about Ida as a youngster, if you're of a mind to hear them. Though I must warn you some of them are sure to embarrass her."

Ida rose from the table, her cheeks now crimson. "Well, there's no time for stories now. I'm sure the shop is full of customers."

"Hardly. Looks like most folks are staying home this morning after hearing what happened at Brewster's place. People are more afraid to bring their children into town on the weekends now. I don't know what's going to happen to the mercantile if these saloons stay in business." She looked at Mick and clamped a hand over her mouth. "Oh, I'm sorry."

"No, don't be. If I've learned anything over the past twenty-four hours, it's that Spring Creek has plenty of activity for the railroad men without another gambling hall going up."

"So you've laid the idea to rest altogether?" Ida looked at him, her eyes bright with excitement.

"I don't know what the future holds." He eased his way out of the chair. "But I don't ever want to see another night like the one we just spent."

He had to face the facts. Looking at these two civilized young women—realizing the challenges they now faced in their once-pristine little town—he suddenly wanted nothing more than to offer them his protection. And, as he looked into Ida's blue eyes, still sparkling at his news, he was tempted to sweep her into his arms, to assure her all would end well, as long as she stuck by him.

The words from Dinah's Bible ran through his mind once more: *In the beginning…*

Sitting here with these two women, Mick Bradley felt as if he might just get his first-ever shot at that. A new beginning.

## Chapter Twenty-Seven

The following Monday afternoon the postman came through town with the mail delivery. Ida spent much of her time at the mercantile sorting through it all. She bundled up stack after stack, much of it for the locals, but quite a bit for The Harvey House, as well.

She tried to remain focused on the task at hand, but found it difficult. With so little sleep the night before, she could barely keep her eyes open, let alone get her work done. And the feelings that arose every time she thought about Mick didn't help, either.

*Lord, I ask you to guide me every step of the way. And, Father, please reveal Yourself to Mick. May he come to know You.*

Dinah came down the stairs moments later with a smile on her face. "You will never guess what I did," she whispered.

After waiting on a customer, Ida turned to respond. "What?"

"I invited Mick to the Fourth of July picnic at the church."

"Oh, Dinah, I don't know—"

"Isn't that the most perfect idea?" Dinah said with a grin. "We've been trying to get him through the doors of the church all along, and if he comes with us to the picnic this Sunday, he will have to attend the service first."

"Well, yes. But I'm not sure this is the best timing for that." Ida chose her words carefully. "After all, he can scarcely get up and down the stairs. How will he make it all the way to the church? It's a good half mile from here."

"I need to take the wagon this Sunday anyway," Dinah explained. "Reverend Langford and several of the men are coming by the store early in the morning to load up barrels and food. And I could never make it on foot with the pies I'm baking."

"Still—"

"Can't you see how the Lord has arranged this?" Dinah's eyes flashed with excitement. "The men can help him down the stairs and onto the wagon. Reverend Langford thinks it's a wonderful idea, and I am inclined to agree, even though I did think of it myself. Now, if only I could figure out a way to get Nellie to agree to come, too. Wouldn't that be a miracle!"

"Of biblical proportions," Ida agreed. Somehow, she could scarcely imagine the saloon girl seated in a pew with a hymnal in hand. Then again, imagining Mick there was nearly as difficult.

"Her shoulder is healing nicely, and she should be able to travel by Sunday." Dinah shrugged. "I will pray about it and see what the Lord does."

"And I will add my prayers to yours," Ida said.

"In the meantime, I've come up with another idea. One I think will help Nellie along on her journey."

"Goodness, Dinah, you are full of ideas this afternoon!"

"Her mother lives alone in Houston and suffers with health problems."

"Yes, so I've heard."

"I think it would be a wonderful idea to bring her here, to Spring Creek. That way she and Nellie can be together. And I've spoken with Doc Klein. He will be able to tend to Mrs. DeVries's needs as well as any of the doctors in the big city."

"But how does Nellie feel about this?" Ida asked. "Does she want her mother to know what she does for a living?"

"I don't know. I haven't mentioned any of this to her yet. But I have laid aside a bit of money for Nellie's mother to travel, if she likes the idea. And they can both stay on here with me. Once Mick is fully healed, I will have plenty of room upstairs. And if I have my way…"

"What?"

"Well, if we could afford it, I would hire Nellie to help around the shop. She's quite good with the customers, and a hard worker at that."

Ida pondered her aunt's generosity. Oh, if only she

could be as good and kind. How did a person get to be so good?

A noise in the stairway distracted them, and Ida looked up, startled to see Mick hobbling down the steps on his crutches.

"What do you think you're doing?" Ida and Dinah spoke in unison.

Ida took several steps in Mick's direction, then slipped an arm around his waist and helped him maneuver the bottom two steps.

His expression changed when she touched him. His look of pain quickly shifted to a look of contentment. She did her best to focus on helping him, and deliberately avoided his eyes. "I can't believe you actually tried to come down those stairs on crutches. You might've fallen."

"Sorry, but I had to get out of that room," he explained. "I couldn't take it anymore." He looked around the store, smiling when he saw several of the local men playing dominoes. "Thought maybe I'd find a game going down here. Looks like I was right."

She helped him over to a chair where he joined in a friendly game with some of the others. Ida returned to her work, but kept a watchful eye on Mick. She listened as laughter rang out across the room when Mick won his first game. Laughter truly was the better medicine.

Later, when the crowd thinned and Dinah had gone upstairs to tend to Nellie, Ida offered Mick a cup of coffee, which he accepted with a smile.

He gestured to an empty chair. "Sit for a minute."

Ida glanced around the store. "All right, just for a minute."

"Believe it or not, I was reading Exodus last night in that Bible Dinah left me." Mick smiled at the look on Ida's face. "Seemed like one minute Pharaoh wanted Moses to stay put. The next, he was chasing him out of town. The whole thing reminded me of, well, myself. My time in Texas. One minute I want to stay, the next I'm ready to go. I can't help but wonder if Spring Creek is my Egypt." He reached out and took her hand. With a twinkle in his eye, he added, "Or maybe it's the Promised Land."

Ida held back a chuckle. So Mick had given thought to what he'd read. The Lord appeared to be moving in his life, drawing him in, wooing him.

After a moment of contemplation, Ida realized that Mick still held her hand. He also held her gaze, which only served to fluster her more. She pulled her hand away, embarrassed.

Ida sighed. Why did she always seem to act like a foolish schoolgirl when Mick was around? As she gazed into his twinkling eyes, she had to admit that acting in a sensible fashion might be out of the question altogether.

Mick watched as Ida placed the Closed sign in the window. Then he inched his way toward the stairwell, knowing he must somehow make it back up to his room. He did not look forward to the challenge.

His broken leg still ached, and the usable one did not appear to be as strong as it once was. Getting down had been difficult enough. How would he manage to get back up?

He tried the first step on his own, using the crutches to lift his weight. Ida approached with a stern look on her face. "Oh, no, you don't. You are not climbing those stairs by yourself."

"Would you mind helping me?"

As she approached, the scent of verbena drew him in. Why did she have to smell like that, anyway? The scent bewitched him almost as much as the tiny bits of blue in her gingham dress that matched her eyes perfectly. Did she have any idea what that could do to a man?

"Careful now," Ida said as she took hold of him at the waist, her hand resting firmly on his back. She gazed up at him with a look that melted his heart.

"I'm always careful." He paused, taking in the color of her hair—the same color as wheat in the summertime. He reached with a fingertip to stroke it and she flinched at his touch, her eyes filling with tears. He gently lifted his hand.

"D-do you still need my help?" she whispered.

"I do." He refused to move. Instead, as he felt her breath against his cheek, he drew her closer still and spoke softly. "I might go on needing it for some time."

"Mick." She shook her head.

"Shh." He put a finger to her lips, then traced it

along her cheek. Instead of pulling away, she closed her eyes. "Do you have any idea what you're doing to me?" he asked in a hoarse whisper.

Ida looked at the ground. Mick leaned down to wrap her in his arms. He felt the trembling in her hands and wondered what she might be thinking, but didn't ask. This wasn't the time for talking.

With his free hand he cupped her chin and she looked up into his eyes. Boldness took over, and he leaned down to press his lips against hers. To his great joy, she wrapped her arms tightly around him, and he wondered if he would ever be the same again.

Seconds later, she slipped from his grasp, her face white as a sheet as she pulled away. "I-I'm sorry."

"I'm not." He whispered the words into her ear.

The jangling of the bell at the door snapped him back to reality. Despite the sign, someone had come in unannounced.

"Ida?" Sophie's voice rang out from beyond the shelves.

Mick tried to take a step up, but lost his balance. Ida steadied him.

"Ida, are you here?"

Ida's face reddened. "I-I'm over here, Sophie," she called out.

He couldn't help but notice the look of desperation in her eyes, as she stepped down onto the floor. For whatever reason, the whole thing made him want to laugh. With common sense taking over, he forced himself to stay calm.

Sophie, who now stood directly in front of the stairwell, looked stunned.

"Sophie, I was just…" Ida took a couple of steps in her friend's direction and reached for the broom once again. "Just cleaning up," she said, crossing away from Sophie.

"Mmm-hmm." Sophie watched Ida, and then looked at Mick. She grinned. "I'll come back another time," she said and made for the door.

At this point, Mick began to chuckle. He plopped down onto the stair on his backside and began to ease his way up one step at a time.

Ida, whose cheeks flamed crimson, continued sweeping, apparently unable to look at him.

Not that he minded. No, indeed. She had given him plenty of attention already, and it had changed his life and his heart forever.

Ida ran from the shop and didn't stop until she reached the railroad tracks. The trembling in her hands hadn't ceased since Mick swept her into his arms.

Why hadn't she pulled away? Why had she allowed herself to be so easily pulled into his web? She'd felt safe in his arms, safer than she would have dared dream.

As she stepped over the tracks, ready to run the rest of the way home, the truth came barreling toward her, like a Great Northern out of control. Somehow, some way…she had fallen for Mick Bradley. Little by little, he had inched his way into her arms, and into her heart.

How Ida would get *this* train to stop, she had no idea.

## Chapter Twenty-Eight

Ida spent Saturday afternoon doing laundry. Her labors gave her plenty of time to think through the events of the day before. Though she tried to forget about how she'd felt in Mick's arms, she couldn't. Oh, how wonderful she'd felt with her head against his shoulder, how safe. And his kiss…

In all her years, she had never known such sweetness. Why then did she feel so guilty? So frightened?

As she did the wash, she pondered what it would be like to have a husband, someone whose clothes she would wash every Saturday and hang on the line to dry.

Ida's cheeks heated up at the very thought.

She tried to focus instead on tomorrow's picnic, making plans for what she would cook later this afternoon. Pies, naturally. And sausage sauerkraut balls, of course. Folks at the church would never let her hear the end of it if she didn't bring her staple. She would also bake several loaves of bread and a hefty cobbler.

Not that she minded bringing so many items. Ida rather enjoyed the attention that went along with her cooking skills. Though she could barely admit it to herself, Ida now hoped to one day have a husband and children to cook for. She could picture it—little ones gathered around the table, clamoring for more of her home cooking.

Ida swatted away a pesky mosquito as she pondered the idea. She'd never imagined herself married until recently.

Until Mick Bradley.

But she couldn't possibly set her sights on him. He was, in every way, her opposite. And yet…

As she recalled his most recent thoughts on the Bible, as she pondered his interest in her cooking, as she thought of his declining interest in building a gambling hall…she could almost see a glimmer of hope.

Still, if such a miracle were to take place, the Lord would surely have to orchestrate every detail…which meant she had to back away and risk losing the one thing she suddenly realized she wanted more than anything else in the world.

Sunday morning, the Fourth of July, dawned bright and clear. Ida found herself in a cheerful state as she prepared for the picnic. Usually she and Papa walked the half mile to the tiny wood-framed church, but they would take the wagon today, what with so many items to carry.

Ida wore her favorite blue dress. She prayed it would stand up to the heat and the outdoor activities. Surely by day's end the puff sleeves would be a bit deflated. Not that she cared, really. On days like this, when folks gathered together to enjoy one another's company, no one much paid attention to such things.

"Time to leave, Ida," her father called.

She went over a checklist in her mind. "I do hope I haven't forgotten anything. It seems I always leave something behind."

Ida stepped up into the wagon to join her father, and they were soon headed toward the church.

"Daughter, I would like to speak with you about something of a serious nature," her father said as they made their way along the dusty road.

"What is it, Papa?" Ida opened her mother's lovely old white parasol to shield herself from the sun. She noticed that her father's cheeks had turned pink, and wondered if perhaps the heat bothered him, too. "Are you not feeling well?" she asked.

"Oh, I am very well. Indeed." The edges of his mustache began to twitch.

"What is it, then?"

"Well—" he snapped the reins to encourage the horses to pick up speed "—I just wanted to tell you something while it's on my mind. And I must confess, I have a lot on my mind this morning."

"What, Papa?"

"Let me start by asking you a question." He kept

his eyes on the road. "How do you feel about the institution of marriage?"

"M-marriage?" Ida's heart quickened. Was he trying to marry her off? "To be honest, in my younger years I never pictured myself married, as most little girls do. I know I'm nearly twenty, but until recently I've never felt…" Instead of completing her sentence, she simply shook her head.

"Never felt you needed a man to sweep in and rescue you?" her father asked. "Like so many other girls?" He laughed. "Don't think I don't know about the plan you made after your mama passed on— never to marry. I've heard bits and pieces of it over the years. Truth is, I feel sure the Lord will one day bring just the right person into your life. If you are open to the idea, that is."

She drew in a deep breath and gave careful thought to her next few words, the sweetness of Mick Bradley's kiss still lingering in her mind. "I am not opposed to the idea of marriage, overall."

"That's good." He turned to give her a smile. "Because I've decided to propose to Myrtle Mae."

"Wh-what?" Ida could hardly believe it. After all, Papa and Myrtle Mae had scarcely had time enough alone to consider the possibility of a romantic union, had they?

Her father's shoulders rose and his chin jutted forward. "I love her, Ida. And she loves me."

"But how do you know?"

Papa laughed. "Oh, trust me, I know. I know what

love looks like. What it feels like." He reached to put his hand on his heart. "When you're in love, everything suddenly makes sense. All the confusion fades away and in its place an undeniable peace settles in your heart."

By that definition, Ida would have to conclude she did *not* love Mick Bradley. Whenever she thought of Mick, peace scattered and confusion took hold. Any future she might have with the man was fraught with complications, no matter how she looked at it.

"I plan to give her a ring at today's picnic, one I secretly ordered from a catalog," Papa said, grinning.

"How did you manage that?" Ida asked, stunned.

"Dinah helped me."

"So Dinah knows about this? A fine kettle of fish this is. My aunt knows before I do. Hardly seems fair."

Her father leaned over and gave her a playful peck on the cheek. "I'd like your permission, Ida, to propose to the woman of my dreams."

"Why, Papa, you're a grown man. You certainly don't need my permission to marry the woman you love."

"I might not need it, but it will comfort me to know we have your blessing."

"Myrtle Mae is a good woman. She will make you a fine wife. And you will eat well, what with both of us here to cook for you."

"And you are fine with that?" Her father gave her an inquisitive look.

Ida laughed. "To be quite honest, I will be happy to have someone to share the responsibilities. Cooking for the lumber-mill workers is quite a challenge, I don't mind saying. And with Myrtle Mae there to help, perhaps I can assist Dinah more. There is much work to be done at the store."

Her father slipped an arm around her shoulder. "I love you, Ida. You've grown into a fine woman, one I'm proud to call my daughter." With a much softer voice, he added, "I'm sure your mother would have been so proud of you. You're very much like her."

Ida blinked away the tears and clutched the parasol a bit tighter. "I often wonder what she would have thought of me."

As they approached the church, Ida's father turned to her. "Pray for me today," he whispered. "I surely hope I can do this."

"You can do it." Ida gave him a pat on the back. "You've achieved so much in your life. No doubt you can handle the likes of one lone woman."

"Oh, I don't know…" Her father gazed out at his bride-to-be. "Some women are enough to make you think you've married three or four."

"At least you'll never be lonely," Ida said with a giggle as the wagon drew to a stop. She looked out over the church property, noticing tables had already been set up outside for the picnic after the service. Several of the local women, Mrs. Weimer included, set food out on the largest one.

Ida looked around, anxious to see if Dinah had arrived yet.

And more anxious still to see if Mick had come with her.

Not until she heard his voice offering to give her a hand did Ida's heart rest. She looked down into his sparkling eyes, and eased her way down from the wagon…landing squarely in his arms.

From the moment Ida Mueller landed in his arms, Mick Bradley committed to attending church every Sunday morning. He would be right here, waiting for her with the same rush of joy that flooded through him now.

Of course, he'd do a better job of assisting the petite beauty if he could throw away the crutches once and for all. As it stood right now, he could barely handle both at once.

Mick released his hold on Ida and reached to grab a flailing crutch. She quickly slipped her arm around his waist.

"Careful now."

He didn't want to be careful. No, Mick wanted to toss caution to the wind, wrap her in his arms and kiss her squarely on the lips, right here in front of her father and all these fine church folks.

On the other hand… He looked up into Mr. Mueller's concerned eyes and stepped back, gripping his crutches a bit tighter. Perhaps waiting would be a better option.

Mick took note of Ida's blue dress and smiled. How would he ever stay focused on the service with her in that dress? "Will you sit with me?" he whispered.

"I don't know." She continued walking, not looking his way. Was she nervous? Worried about what folks were thinking?

Sure enough, he noticed the stares of others nearby and wondered if they could see into his heart. If so, they surely knew he must sit next to this woman or die trying. He continued easing his way along on the crutches, wishing he could be rid of them forever. Would this leg never heal? If not, would she even look twice at him?

"I suppose it would be proper, as long as Papa joins us," Ida whispered back.

He reached over and took her hand, giving it a squeeze. She squeezed back then released it quickly.

As Mick reached the door of the building, Reverend Langford met him with a handshake. "So glad you could join us. Welcome."

Mick offered an abrupt nod. After skimming through that Bible Dinah had left on his bedside table, there were a number of things he'd like to discuss with his reverend friend. Perhaps they could wait until a later date. Likely, Reverend Langford would come by for a visit one day this week, anyway. Then, in the privacy of his room, Mick could ask the primary question that had bothered him all week— or most of his life, depending on how you looked at it. If God loved him as much as the Bible said He did, why did He allow the tragedies of the past few weeks? The fire. The attack. His injuries.

And why had God allowed his parents to be taken from him at such a young age? Surely the Almighty could have prevented their deaths. Instead, He'd left a young boy alone in the world without anyone to tend to his needs except his brother, and strangers. A more merciful God would've kept his parents alive, right?

Pushing aside all such morbid questions, Mick allowed Ida and her father to help him up the stairs. He entered the tiny building with its rough-hewn pews and looked around, surprised at what he saw. "This is nothing like the churches in Chicago."

"Oh?" Ida gave him a curious look.

He shrugged. "I only remember the church my mother took me to as a child, and it was all stained glass and steeples, that sort of thing. The pews were polished to perfection. This place is—" he glanced around, taking note of the small, plain space "—very homey."

Ida smiled. "It's not that we're opposed to fancy buildings. I saw a few in Houston, and they were quite breathtaking." She looked around the room with a smile. "But I grew up in this little church and it suits me just fine."

As they sat in a pew near the front, Mick wondered what his mother would've thought of this place. He somehow felt she would love it here.

Two women came in and looked down their noses at Mick. He heard one of them whisper, "What's he doing here, anyway?" The other one quieted her. "Shush, Cora. Maybe the Lord wants to do business with him."

Had the Lord brought him here to perform some sort of business transaction? A feeling of discomfort slithered over Mick. What was it about churchgoers, anyway—always trying to get folks to change their ways. What made them think their way was best?

Before he could think about this any longer, Myrtle Mae sat at the piano and began to play a hymn, one he vaguely remembered from childhood. He couldn't seem to recall the words, but the melody...

Mick closed his eyes and could almost see himself, a youngster of six or seven, standing with his mother's hand tightly clasped in his own, singing.

Ah, yes. As the residents of Spring Creek rose and began to sing "Tell Me the Old, Old Story," Mick opened his eyes and listened with interest, the words coming back to him in full force.

Tell me the old, old story of unseen things above,
Of Jesus and His glory, of Jesus and His love.
Tell me the story simply, as to a little child,
For I am weak and weary, and helpless and
defiled.

He looked over at Ida, watching as she sang the words in a voice as clear as any angel could boast. Like the songwriter, Mick understood feelings of weakness and weariness. The past few weeks had taken their toll. Every inch of his journey had worn him down a bit more. And despite his best attempts to appear strong, he felt completely helpless, just as the song said.

And now, as he attempted to stand, his heart reacted to the haunting melody. It reminded him far too much of his mother—a memory he couldn't bear, the pain of her loss still so deep. The parishioners carried on.

Tell me the story slowly, that I may take it in,
That wonderful redemption, God's remedy for sin.
Tell me the story often, for I forget so soon;
The early dew of morning has passed away at noon.
Tell me the same old story when you have cause to fear
That this world's empty glory is costing me too dear.
Yes, and when that world's glory is dawning on my soul,
Tell me the old, old story: "Christ Jesus makes thee whole."

*Empty glory* reminded Mick of his now-empty lot. And that line about Jesus making you whole made him think of something Reverend Langford had said the first day they'd met. *You can put yer boots in the oven, but that don't make 'em biscuits.*

The pain in Mick's leg intensified, to the point

where he ached to sit. He tried to shift his weight, but found himself more uncomfortable than ever.

As Mick finally gave in and eased his way down into the pew, he pondered the dilemma he now faced. At this point, he couldn't be sure which bothered him more—his leg, or his still-empty heart.

# Chapter Twenty-Nine

Out of the corner of her eye, Ida kept a watchful eye on Mick. She could tell the song was affecting him. His entire demeanor changed the moment Myrtle Mae's fingers hit the keys.

Longing took hold of Ida's heart as she realized what surely must be taking place, and she whispered up a silent prayer for the Lord to somehow woo Mick into His arms. While she had once thought his salvation an impossible task, even for the Almighty, Ida now pleaded for that very thing. She approached the Lord in a humble state of mind, asking Him to forgive her for ever having doubted His love for Mick. What an arrogant, narrow-minded girl she had been, to think the Creator wouldn't be bothered with a gambling-hall man.

She sang the final words to the song. *Tell me the old, old story, Christ Jesus makes thee whole.*

The old Ida—the prideful, biased one—spent the next few moments allowing God to do just that. The fears and failings she had struggled with in the past dissipated as the final notes to the song were played. And by the time she took her seat next to Mick, Ida truly felt the words taking root in her heart.

She listened with renewed interest as Reverend Langford delivered his sermon, using the Fourth of July as the foundation for a powerful message on liberty in Christ. Though she had known the Lord from childhood, had given her heart to Him as a youngster, something about today's words stirred her heart anew.

Just a few lines into his text, a rustle at the back of the building caught Ida's attention. She looked back to discover the door flung wide and Nellie DeVries standing there, arm in a cloth sling, a nervous look on her face. Reverend Langford interrupted his message to welcome her at once, and she eased her way in, looking for a familiar face.

Thankfully, Dinah caught Nellie's eye and waved for the frightened young woman to join her. As Dinah scooted over to make room, Ida noticed Johnsey Fischer seated next to her. She caught Dinah's eye and smiled.

Reverend Langford continued on with his message, the words ringing clear across the sanctuary. The resounding theme of the morning—Christ's ability to heal His weary, wounded children from the sins of their past, and the resulting liberty when one placed one's trust in Jesus's work on the cross. A liberty far more precious than any Fourth of July celebration, and one that involved a chorus of angels singing with heavenly gusto.

The weeping started quietly at first. But as the message reached its peak, Nellie's sniffles evolved into full-fledged sobs. Ida wanted to wrap the young woman in her arms. When she looked over her shoulder, she noted that Dinah had already taken care of that.

Myrtle Mae approached the piano for the final hymn, and the congregation rose to sing. Ida wasn't sure which made the stronger impression on her heart—the undeniable glistening in Mick Bradley's eyes, or the wails coming from the pew behind her.

The service drew to an end, and Mick breathed a sigh of relief. Unlike Nellie, he had resisted the urge to go to the front for prayer as the final song concluded. No, he would rather do business with God—if that was truly what was happening—on his own. One private step at a time. And, no matter how much Reverend Langford turned up the heat, Mick still wasn't sure he was ready to pull his boots out of the oven.

Not that he owned any boots.

The message had served to shift his attention away from his problems for a few minutes, at least. His animosity toward Brewster, his ever-present thoughts about the investors—somehow they'd all taken a back seat to Reverend Langford's powerful words.

Ida excused herself to help set up for the picnic. Mick took the opportunity to visit with Mr. Mueller. However, the older fellow looked a bit off-kilter today. Pale, even.

"Are you not feeling well?" Mick asked.

"Oh, fine." Mr. Mueller pressed his hands into his pockets and looked to the front of the sanctuary. Mick followed his gaze, noting Myrtle Mae rising from the piano bench with sheet music in her hands. Ida's father eased his way through the crowd to offer his assistance.

So that was it. The man had his eye on a woman. And in church, at that.

Well, could any less be said of Mick? Though he'd listened to Reverend Langford's sermon, his mind had wandered a time or two to the gorgeous woman on his left. And who could blame him? His heart felt as if it would leap from his chest every time Ida opened her mouth to sing.

Easing his way around on his crutches, Mick turned and found Johnsey standing behind him. Happy to see a familiar face, Mick smiled and shook his hand.

"What did you think?" Johnsey asked as they made their way toward the door.

"Not quite what I was expecting. I rather imagined more red-faced shouting, that sort of thing."

Johnsey laughed. "It's hard for me to picture God hollering at folks, so it never makes much sense when I see preachers doing it."

Mick pondered his friend's words before adding, "Well, I guess I just figured God was in the shouting business. Never knew the difference."

Johnsey offered his assistance, and before long they had reached the bottom of the front stairs. Colorful quilts dotted the church lawn, the patches of vibrant blues, whites and yellow providing a nice contrast against the green grass and the shade trees overhead. The hot afternoon sun blazed down on them, and he longed for a breeze to blow through.

Mick watched as Ida prepared a spot off in the distance. Dinah was spreading a quilt next to hers, so he and Johnsey headed in that direction.

"Looks like we're both thinking the same thing," Johnsey said with a laugh.

Mick nodded. "I don't mind admitting, she's done something to me."

"You've got it bad, haven't you?" Johnsey slapped him on the back and chuckled. "I know just how you feel. As far as I'm concerned, Dinah is manna from heaven."

Mick watched as Ida interacted with Carter and the other children. Listened to their voices raised in song as she led them on a Pied Piper trail around and through the pine trees.

A woman like that could certainly get under a man's skin.

Johnsey went to sit with Dinah, and Mick made his way through the throng of people to Ida's side, happy when she turned to him with a welcoming smile.

Reverend Langford called for everyone's attention and led the group in a prayer before the meal.

Then the real fun began. Folks gathered in long lines to fill their plates. Mick willingly agreed to let Johnsey fetch his plate for him, and stretched out on the blue and white quilt underneath a canopy of pine trees, alongside Ida and her father. And Myrtle Mae, of course.

Mick kept a watchful eye on several things. Ida, who seemed more than a little giddy today. Her father, who acted like a nervous cat. Myrtle Mae, who gabbed with Emma Gertsch about those ridiculous dime novels—the same ones he'd secretly taken to reading. And Nellie, who talked quietly with Dinah about her ailing mother in Houston.

After eating his fill of Emma's homemade pickles, Myrtle Mae's fried chicken, baked beans from the reverend's wife and plenty of Ida's lemon meringue pie, Mick settled back to watch the entertainment. A couple of the men, including Sophie's father, stood with fiddles in their hands and began tuning them. Within minutes, hands were clapping, toes were tapping and several of the children had taken to skipping beneath the pines, their merry voices reverberating against the dense forest behind them. My, but these Texans sure knew how to throw a nice lawn party.

Mick took a sip of his lemonade and looked at the crew of people gathered around him on the quilt, his heart feeling as though it might burst at any moment. They looked for all the world like family…a family he could learn to love.

A startling idea entered Mick's mind, one he could not ignore. The more he chewed on it, the more he realized it made perfect sense. Within a few minutes the idea grew into a workable plan, a perfectly wonderful one. Why hadn't he thought of it before?

Mick leaned back and contemplated the idea rolling around in his head. It had come from somewhere. The Lord, perhaps? Anything was possible.

Maybe, just maybe, Mick could pay his investors back by September after all.

If he could just get the townspeople to join him—and keep a secret.

Ida finished up a plate of ham and baked beans, and offered her remaining piece of chicken to Johnsey, who gladly accepted it. Then she took a sliver of lemon meringue pie, eating it slowly. The sun hung bright and heavy above them, and she felt herself perspiring. Glistening, as Dinah called it. Thankfully, she'd chosen a spot underneath the trees to place their quilt. The shade provided a bit of relief.

She looked over to the Weimers' quilt and saw Sophie watching her. Ida lifted a hand in greeting, but did not get up to say hello. Sophie waved back, a strange look on her face. Ida felt uneasy for reasons she could not explain. There was something between them, something she could not identify. A tension…

Once the fiddlers got to fiddling, Ida leaned back against a tree and closed her eyes. Her mind wandered—until the music came to an abrupt, unexpected halt. She heard a giggle of embarrassment from Myrtle Mae. Ida's eyes flew open at once, and she saw her papa on bended knee in front of the woman he loved, his hand tightly clasping hers. Even from here, Ida could see the trembling.

He reached into his pocket and came out with a slender silver ring, which he held up for all to see. "I want my friends and neighbors to witness this," he said in a resounding voice. "I am a man in love."

Myrtle Mae's cheeks reddened and she let out another giggle. All across the churchyard, folks quieted their conversations and turned in rapt attention.

Ida couldn't help but laugh, too. Her papa looked his bride-to-be in the eye as he spoke tenderly. "Myrtle Mae, I love you. I'd shout it from the treetops, if I thought it wouldn't embarrass you."

"It wouldn't." She gave him a wink.

He nodded then finished up his little speech. "I'm askin' you to be my bride. Will you marry me, Myrtle Mae? Put me out of my misery once and for all. Say you'll be mine."

She nodded and whispered a tearful, "Yes." A roar of applause rose up from the crowd.

Myrtle Mae got her ring.

Papa got his bride-to-be.

And Ida…well, from where she sat, the only thing more appealing than the scene before her was the look in the eye of the man who reached over and took hold of her hand, giving it a squeeze.

With joy flooding her heart, she squeezed back.

## Chapter Thirty

"Did you save room for cobbler, Mr. Bradley?"

Emma Gertsch's words certainly got Mick's attention. He opened his eyes and looked at the older woman in curiosity.

"Cobbler?"

"Yes indeed." She rose to her feet and brushed the dirt from her dress. "It's our annual cobbler bakeoff and we'll be needing judges."

Though he wanted to groan, his stomach already painfully full from the meal he'd just consumed, Mick thought better of it. "Am I to assume you've entered a cobbler in the bakeoff?"

"Well, now that you mention it…" She fanned herself. "But I would never stoop to persuading you to vote for mine. That would be wrong. Though I must say the dewberries from my property are the juiciest in the county and I do spend hours collecting them each spring."

"I see."

From behind him, Ida laughed. "You have nothing to fear, Mick. None of the entries are marked, so you won't have any idea whose is whose. I've entered a cobbler myself."

Mick looked over at Johnsey and patted his full stomach. With a laugh, Johnsey stood and helped Mick to his feet.

Fifteen minutes and a dozen bites later, Mick and Johnsey declared a tasty peach cobbler the winner. Truly, Mick didn't know when he'd ever tasted anything so fine. He prayed the flavorful concoction belonged to Ida. A blue ribbon would go a long way toward winning her heart. Unfortunately, Myrtle Mae bounded to the front of the crowd to claim her ribbon, a tenacious smile on her face.

"Looks like it's been your day," Reverend Langford said, handing her the ribbon. "Not quite sure how you're going to top this one!"

"Oh, we'll top it, all right." She turned her attention to the crowd. "We'll be having the weddin' soon, and I'll bake up the tastiest cake you ever did see. We'll celebrate together." She turned to face her husband-to-be as she asked, "How does an autumn ceremony sound to you?"

"If I can wait that long." He winked and reached for her hand.

"We look forward to that," Reverend Langford said.

As Mick moved back in Ida's direction, he thought about the upcoming wedding. He wondered what it would be like to settle here, marry Ida and raise a family.

The longer he thought about those things, the more plausible they became. Within minutes, he felt as though his heart might spring from his chest. Could he really do it? Live here in Texas? Maybe he'd been right when he compared Spring Creek to the Promised Land, especially in light of the new plan that now consumed his thoughts. Perhaps that's what the Lord had had in mind all along.

Ida worked alongside Dinah, packing her aunt's wagon. With so many things to return to the mercantile, she thought it best to offer a hand. Besides, a ride into town meant a few more minutes with Mick, something she dearly craved—even if he hadn't voted for her apple cobbler.

Still, in spite of her growing feelings, Ida knew better than to give her heart just yet. She sensed that the Lord had quite a bit of work to do in Mick's life, and she certainly didn't want to get in the way of that. Too much too fast could have devastating consequences. To put the cart ahead of the horse—especially in matters of the heart—was never a good idea.

A short time later they arrived at the mercantile, and Ida looked on with a smile as Johnsey helped Dinah down from the wagon. After all the sadness Dinah had endured, she deserved the kind of happiness a man like Johnsey could bring.

Ida turned and looked at the empty lot next door. Though she didn't want to see it used for a gambling hall, she had to admit that the charred ruins made her sad. And the look in Mick's eyes every time he gazed at the property nearly broke her heart. *Lord, lead the way. Show him what to do. Show us all what to do.*

"A penny for your thoughts."

Ida swung around, unable to hide her grin as she saw Mick standing close by. "Oh, I was just thinking about Dinah and Johnsey."

He glanced up to see them disappear into the store. "They make quite the couple, don't they?"

"Yes," Ida agreed, "though I never saw it coming, if you want to know the truth of it. They seem so different. And he's nothing like Larson, in any respect." In fact, Ida didn't know when she'd seen two more different men. Larson had been older than his years, an average-looking man with a heart as big as Texas. Johnsey's wide smile invited others in, and almost made them forget about his wholesome good looks and boyish face.

"I've always heard that opposites attract." Mick drew a bit closer, and Ida felt her breath catch in her throat.

"True," she whispered, "though I cannot help but think that any romantic union would be unduly strained if the parties were vastly different."

"Different, as in a big-city gambling-hall man and a small-town girl who is more at home on a church pew than a bar stool?" His eyes twinkled with mischief, but Ida struggled to find the humor in his words.

"I thought you'd laid the idea of a gambling hall to rest, Mick."

"I'm not saying otherwise. It's just interesting to think I've come all the way to Texas looking for one thing," he said with a pensive look, brushing a loose hair out of her face, "and ended up with another."

"Another?" *Is he referring to...me?*

He looked toward the empty lot. "My original plans lie in ruins."

Ida followed his gaze. No doubt, giving up on his dream had come at a cost, but he needed to let go of that altogether, or she could never consider marrying him.

Marrying him? Where had such a notion come from? Mick Bradley had never even asked to court her, let alone offer a marriage proposal. Surely the heat must be playing with her thoughts today. She took a step backward.

Mick gave her a curious look. "What did you think of that sermon this morning?"

"I enjoyed it immensely. Reverend Langford always manages to tie his messages in to the holidays, and I thought his liberty theme was quite brilliant. Of course, I always love to hear his testimony. He is quite a changed man. Gives me hope."

"For me?"

She smiled. "For people in general, I mean. Myself included."

"I guess it's going to take a while for the Almighty to convince me He's got a grandiose plan for my life. Seems like the only thing He's shown me so far is, well, ashes."

"There's a wonderful scripture about God's ability to bring beauty from ashes," Ida said. "And I've no doubt He will do that for you, if you ask Him to."

"He's already brought one good thing from the rubble," Mick said. "I never would have known you—really known you—if not for the attack I've come under."

"True."

After a pause, he added, "But don't you see? That's my dilemma. I'm having a hard time trusting in a God who allowed something like that to happen. He could have stopped it. For that matter, He could've stopped Brewster and his men from burning down my business. A lot of money went into that lumber, and the money I paid the workers, too. Just doesn't make sense to me. If the Lord wanted to stop me in my tracks he should have done it before I made the investment." Mick shrugged.

"There are so many things about God's timing—and His will—that elude me," Ida confessed. "He could have stopped Larson's death. And the death of my mother." She drew in a deep breath. "We cannot comprehend why things happen like they do, but we trust anyway."

Mick shrugged. "That might make sense to you, but from where I stand it seems mighty impractical to put my trust in a God who's liable to derail me. Brewster's men nearly took my life, Ida. That's enough to make me angry. And even angrier that they still haven't been brought to justice."

"Our system of justice is vastly different from the Lord's," she countered. "'Vengeance is mine, saith the Lord. I will repay.'"

"It might be His," Mick agreed, "but that doesn't stop me from wanting to take matters into my own hands sometimes."

"You must trust me when I say that I understand all too well," she said. "I've always been one to rush out ahead of God. To take things into my own hands when they belong in His. But if I've learned one thing over the past couple of months it is that we're sometimes called to give God the reins. Even when it doesn't make sense."

Mick shook his head. "Sounds easy enough, but hearing it and doing it are two different things."

"Of course." Ida gave him a concerned look. "I do hope you will allow the Lord to continue to work in your heart, Mick. You've made such headway, and I know what a strong man you are. You will be stronger still if you make your peace with God."

"I suppose." He pulled her close. "But why do we need to talk about all of that right now? Isn't it enough that we're together?" He leaned in and whispered gently in her ear, "You've stolen my heart, Ida. Do you understand what I'm saying? I'm undone."

Ida felt a lump rise in her throat and she dreaded speaking her next words. "My feelings for you are very strong, as well. But it's not enough, Mick, though I'm sure this won't make much sense to you.

I cannot give my heart to a man who has not given *his* heart to the Lord."

"I'm trying to figure all that out, but it's going to take some time. I'm on the right track, don't you think?" He gave her a pleading look. "I'm plenty willing to admit I've got a ways to go before I get things all figured out. But I don't see why that has to keep us from being together."

"It's a matter of wholly submitting your will. Asking Him to be Lord of your life."

"I'm just not sure what that entails."

She smiled. "It means He takes control. And it means you have to be willing to trade in your dreams for His, if that makes sense. Once that takes place, I'm more than happy to—" she felt her cheeks flush "—consider courting you. If that's what you're asking."

"Yes, that's what I'm asking." Mick rested against his crutches. "But I wonder if you're hesitant for another reason."

"What do you mean?"

"Maybe you don't want a man who's crippled. Is that the real issue here?"

Her heart broke at his painful words. Clearly, he did not understand. "You're not crippled in the usual way," Ida said. "It's not your bones that haven't mended—it's your heart. And until it does, until you've made your peace with God, I cannot…"

"Cannot what?"

"Cannot allow myself to consider the possibility. It's not enough that you care for me."

"You care for me, too."

"I do care for you." She swallowed the growing lump in her throat. "But God's plan is bigger than what I'm feeling. Or what you're feeling, for that matter."

"How do you know that?"

"Because I know that it will bring a peace that passes all understanding, and I don't have that. Not yet." She gave him an imploring look. "I want to have it, and I'm praying for God's perfect will in this situation."

A defiant look came into Mick's eyes and he pulled back, his jaw tightening. "Well, when you figure that out, come and tell me, because I can honestly say I don't have a clue what all the fuss is about. I'm crazy about you, and I know you love me, too." He paused and seemed to be collecting his thoughts. "You're a stubborn girl."

"What?"

"You've got a backbone of steel, like those railroad tracks over there. No bending, no concessions. And yet you would have me concede all my plans, my dreams." He shook his head. "Where is the fairness in that?"

Tears sprang to Ida's eyes as she spoke. "This isn't about what's fair, Mick. It's about what's right."

"I only know one thing that's right." He turned back toward the mercantile, stumbling on his crutches as he mumbled, "And you're about to let it slip right through your fingers."

# Chapter Thirty-One

The following afternoon Mick called for Ida to meet him upstairs in the kitchen. He needed her assistance with a project, one he could not unveil just yet. He knew his unusual request would upset her, but figured it would be worth the risk, especially if everything went as planned. She entered the room cautiously.

"Did you want me, Mick?" She wiped her hands on her apron.

*More than you know.*

"The shop is full of customers and Dinah needs my help," she said.

Indeed, something about Dinah seemed amiss today. He'd noticed it early on. Her eyes had a misty glow about them, a sure sign that she'd been crying. And a somber expression replaced her usually bright countenance. Something felt wrong.

"Nellie's gone for the day," Ida continued. "She took the morning train to Houston to fetch her mother."

"I see." After a brief pause, he continued. "Well, I am sorry to interrupt, but this will only take a moment. I wonder if you would be so kind as to call for your father. I have a business matter to discuss with him."

"Papa?"

"Yes."

"Is this about lumber?" The expression on her face hardened as she spoke the words.

"Perhaps." Mick offered up a smile as he thought about his new plans. A visit from Mr. Mueller would prove to be essential, as would some private time with Johnsey and Dinah. And the local banker. Yes, with the help of others, his dream of a new building would become a reality.

Ida crossed her arms. "I could call for Papa if you like, but it hurts my heart to do so."

"I beg your pardon?"

"I suspect that you are reconsidering the gambling hall. Hoping to acquire funds to rebuild?"

"Well, to be honest…" How much should he tell her?

"Mick, I just think it's a bad idea, especially now." Her eyes misted over and he wondered at her sudden outburst of emotion.

How could he begin to explain his motives if she resorted to tears? Standing up to a tearful woman had never been his forte.

Ida's features hardened before he could say a word. "Mick Bradley, I'm ashamed of you."

"Excuse me?" Would she not even let him get a word in edgewise?

Her cheeks now flamed. "The Lord has spared your life. Given you a second chance. And you're going to take advantage of that by returning to the very thing that drove you from Him in the first place? Don't you see? Building that place will be your ruin."

He was more frustrated than ever. Obviously, she didn't care to listen to his explanation, though he had carefully planned just how he would break the news. "Apparently, speaking with you about this is useless, at least right now. Maybe we can talk again later."

"I'm begging you to reconsider. This is not the direction you should be headed. Remember what you said about the Promised Land?"

He nodded. "Of course."

"Only good things await people in the promised land," she emphasized.

"But how do you know what I'm contemplating?" he asked. "What makes you think it's bad?" Honestly, if she would just slow down, he would convince her that his motives and his actions were anything but.

"I can't see into your heart."

"Well, that's a shame." He shook his head. "I'm convinced you would change your mind if you could." Indeed, she would put an end to this arguing right away.

Mick tried to stand, but lost his balance as the bad leg gave way beneath him. She rushed to his side, and caught him as he started to go down. They stood in a tight embrace, her flushed cheeks now at his shoulder level.

He glanced down into her tear-filled eyes and for a brief moment wanted to draw her close, wanted to trace a tear down her cheek with his fingertip, wanted to run his hands through that beautiful blond hair. If he told her everything would work out fine in the end, would she believe it? He had the urge to kiss her on the spot—surely that would leave a much better memory than bickering.

He managed a few words, whispering into her ear. "It seems you're always saving me from falling."

"I'd like to save you again," she whispered back. "But only the Lord can do that. And I pray you will open your heart to Him and allow it. You must see that building the gambling hall is in direct opposition to His will. Please don't do this, Mick."

"Ida, calm yourself." He eased back down onto the chair once again, dejected. "Just call for your papa and I will fill you in on the details later. In the meantime, I'm just going to have to ask you to trust me. Can you do that? I know I haven't given you much reason to do so in the past, but you will find that I am trustworthy, I assure you."

She stood in strained silence, her cheeks flushed. Ida's emotional response had shaken him to his core. Why would she respond in such a way? Had she really noticed no change in his life—his attitude—at all?

She went back downstairs to the store, and within an hour, Mr. Mueller arrived. Mick gave the best presentation he could manage, speaking animatedly about the revenue his new building would bring to the community. If Mr. Mueller would just see fit to front him the lumber, that was.

."Young feller, I don't see as you're in any shape to be building anything. Looks to me like you should be recuperating, not working."

"I can do both," Mick argued. "And I plan to stay put in Spring Creek. If you'll do me the favor of trusting me with the lumber up front, that is. If you don't…" Mick couldn't finish the statement. He had no idea what he'd do if this plan fell through.

Mr. Mueller's face softened and the crinkles around his eyes deepened as a smile lit his face. "You're doing this for my girl, aren't you?"

"I am, sir." Mick did his best not to let the grin spread too far. He wanted Ida's father to take his request seriously, after all.

"I take that to mean you love her." Dirk Mueller's mustache twitched.

"I do, sir."

"Well, in that case, how could I possibly say no?" The older man gave Mick a bear hug, and patted him on the back. "If you love her half as much as I think you do, she's going to be one happy woman. Now let's get busy and build that building!"

Ida made the journey toward home as the sun began to set. She drew in one deep breath after another, trying to remain calm and levelheaded. Only one problem—she didn't want to remain calm. She wanted to scream. To kick something. To shout to the skies, "Once a wolf, always a wolf!"

Mick Bradley. What had she ever seen in the man? And whatever made her think he'd change, just to make her happy? Had he been toying with her emotions all along? Did he own a host of gambling halls from North to South? Was there an Ida in every town between here and Chicago?

Just the thought of it sent a shiver down her spine. "I should have heeded my own warnings," she muttered under her breath as she drew near the tracks. Yes, dressed in sheep's clothing he'd somehow wormed his way into her heart. And she'd let him. Simple as that. She had no one but herself to blame. Somehow, knowing that made her even more angry.

"Ida!"

Ida turned and saw Sophie coming toward her.

"I missed you at the mercantile. Dinah told me you'd just left," Sophie said, trying to catch her breath. "Is Dinah all right? She looked quite sad."

"Yes, something is not right with Dinah today. She wouldn't talk about it, however."

"I see."

They continued on in silence for a moment.

"Did you enjoy the picnic yesterday?" Sophie asked.

"I did. I'm sorry we didn't get a chance to speak," Ida said. "I was…"

Sophie waited for her to continue. When Ida didn't, Sophie smiled.

"Ida, I want to talk to you about Mick."

Ida was surprised by the rush of jealousy that came over her. The words flew out of her mouth before she could stop them. "Sophie, I know that you think Mick is very handsome. You've made no secret of that. But you must know that he is not the man we would wish him to be. He is planning—"

Sophie put her hand on her friend's arm. "I think you've misinterpreted my feelings. Yes, he is a handsome man, but I'm not interested in him. I never have been. Ida, I've known you a very long time. Almost our entire lives. And I feel I must tell you that I have never seen you look at a man the way you look at Mick Bradley. All those comments I made about him were just my way of trying to get you to see him, Ida. To truly see him. To look beyond his gambling hall and see the way he looks at you. He's never had eyes for anyone in this town but you, Ida. Don't doubt that for a minute."

Ida was so stunned by her friend's words that she couldn't come up with a reply.

"Please, Ida, don't let this chance pass you by. Mick is a good man. Even if he is a bit misguided at times." Sophie pulled Ida into a hug. "Life is full of wonderful opportunities but you have to recognize them in order to take advantage. Do not miss this one because you've got blinders on."

Ida wiped a tear from her cheek as Sophie released her. Sophie gave her hand a final squeeze and headed toward her home. Ida stood frozen in place, speechless.

What a fool she'd been. Her best friend had probably known how she felt about Mick long before she herself did. And to think that Sophie would try to win Mick for herself was absurd. Had Ida no faith in their friendship? She felt she scarcely knew herself anymore.

She began to walk. As she came upon the railroad tracks, she had a sudden realization and a wave of guilt washed over her. July 5. Larson had died two years ago today in this very spot. No wonder Dinah had looked so somber today. That one night had changed everything for Dinah—for all of them. These tracks served as an ever-present reminder. And yet, Dinah was falling in love. She was allowing herself to fall for Johnsey Fischer—she was moving forward and taking a chance, trusting in her feelings.

*Can I not do the same? Is God showing me a path, showing me His will—and I'm ignoring the signs?*

Ida looked down at the tracks in front of her. With a deep breath, she lifted her foot and took a step across.

As soon as Dirk Mueller left the mercantile, Mick started putting together a plan for how—and when— the new building would come together. And just how he would let Ida know. Sooner was probably better than later, given her earlier response.

He summoned Dinah to his room. Mick smiled at the look of hopeful expectation in her eyes when he gave her the particulars of his new plan, and her excitement seemed to grow when he asked if she would send word for the reverend to come tomorrow. She scurried off with a smile on her face—the first he'd seen all day.

Ida's words came rushing back to him after Dinah left. *"It's not your bones that haven't mended—it's your heart. And until it does, until you've made your peace with God..."*

The words had felt like an accusation at the time, but now they blanketed him, bringing hope. In spite of his failings, Mick wanted to believe the Lord could change things, turn things around. Could God do that...for him? For his relationship with Ida?

Maybe his train needed to be on a different track, headed off in a completely different direction.

The words to the hymn Mick had sung last Sunday came back, stirring his heart to action.

Tell me the story, as to a little child,
For I am weak and weary, and helpless and defiled.

Mick looked down at his leg, and then shifted his gaze to the crutches leaning up against the chair. He believed now that his leg would mend in time. Someday he would look back on all this as nothing more than a distant memory.

Oh, but when he thought of Ida—when he re-membered the way she'd felt in his arms, heard again the sound of her voice as she chided him, thought about the sparkle in her blue eyes, the determination in her voice—he could hardly contain himself. This was a girl sent straight from heaven. What was the word Johnsey had used? Manna. Yes, manna from heaven. And he would win her over with this new plan, for he'd placed her in the very center of it.

He'd made other plans in the past, and things had ended badly. When he'd been in charge, the situation had spiraled out of control.

What could he do to prevent that from happening this time around? Only one thing came to mind—the one thing he'd avoided most of his adult life. With a heavy but hopeful heart, Mick Bradley bowed his head and began to pray.

## Chapter Thirty-Two

Ida arrived at the mercantile at exactly two o'clock for once. She found the place busier than usual. There seemed to be an excitement in the air— something she couldn't put her finger on, exactly. For one thing, Dinah looked surprisingly happy today. More so than usual, in light of her sober countenance yesterday.

"What's happening here?" Ida asked as she reached for her apron. "Papa's been whistling all afternoon, and you've got a smile that would light up the town."

"Do I?"

"You do. So fess up. What's going on?"

Dinah shrugged. "I don't know what you mean."

Ida fussed with her apron strings. "I figured you'd be overwhelmed, what with Nellie and Johnsey both being gone."

Ida glanced out the window at the throng of people passing by. Sure, the train from up North had brought in newcomers. Likely they'd venture into the store before heading on to their final destinations. "What time do you expect Nellie and her mama?"

"Any time now. I've got their room ready upstairs. And Johnsey will be in on the afternoon train with his father. I'm looking forward to meeting him in person—I've heard so much about him."

Ida nodded, her gaze shifting toward the stairs. She longed to ask about Mick, but didn't want to appear anxious. What in the world had Mick said to her father to put such a spring in his step and song in his heart?

"Yes, he's still here."

"What?" Ida turned to face her aunt.

"I'm guessing you were thinking of Mick," Dinah whispered, "and he's still here for another few days."

"And then?"

"I'm not sure of his plans, only that he said he will stay through the end of the week. And in the meantime, he's holding court with someone up there."

Ida felt her stomach knot up. "Papa?"

"Your father is expected to return any moment," Dinah explained, "but right now Mick is busy talking to—"

"Excuse me, miss, I wonder if you could point me toward the soda crackers." An unfamiliar railroad worker interrupted their conversation. Ida led him to the aisle with the soda crackers, wondering about Mick's visitor.

Papa soon arrived and headed up the stairs. If Ida

hadn't been so busy, she would have been tempted to march up there and find out what was going on.

Nellie and her mother arrived at two-thirty, and were welcomed at once. Dinah ushered them up the stairs, taking the frail woman's bags and offering encouraging smiles. Nellie looked hopeful and nervous. Ida imagined she was longing for her mother to be well and whole, for this new venture to work.

After getting them settled in, Dinah returned with a shimmer in her eyes. Very rarely did Ida see her aunt cry.

"Is everything all right?" she whispered.

Her aunt turned back with a shrug. "I don't know how long Nellie will have her mother with her on this earth, is all. And it put me in mind of my mama. And yours." She brushed away a tear and went back to work. Ida did her best to pay attention to the customers, but Dinah's words had touched a deep place in her heart, one she hadn't visited for some time.

She did long for her mother, more than she'd admitted. Somehow it helped to know that Dinah— a spiritual giant in Ida's eyes—struggled with the same feelings. Together, they would help Nellie through this. Whatever time the dear girl had with her mother would be spent happily.

At quarter till three, a voice at the front door rang out in exaggerated volume, causing everyone in the place to look up in surprise.

"Dinah Mueller."

Ida looked across the room and noticed Johnsey

standing there alongside an older man. Carter, who sat on the floor playing with his marbles, scrambled to his feet and ran to Johnsey, leaping into his arms with joy written all over his face.

"Well, hello there, son." Johnsey gave him a warm hug then placed the youngster back on the ground. "I'd spend more time saying hello, but I've got some business to take care of with your mother." Johnsey eased his way through the heavy crowd and drew near the register.

"You cut in line, sir," Dinah said with an embarrassed smile.

"Mmm-hmm."

"Can I help you?"

"You can. Come on around here to this side of the register."

She looked at the crowd of people and shook her head. "I have customers to wait on."

The folks in line all eased their way back, likely curious to see what Johnsey would do next. He strode behind the register and met her face-to-face.

She looked up at him with whimsy in her eyes. "You're up to something."

"I am." He put his hands around her slender waist and lifted her to sit on the heavy glass showcase.

Dinah gasped and her cheeks pinked. "Put me down from here," she said in a whisper. "What are you doing?"

"Exactly what the Lord placed on my heart to do." Reaching into his pocket, he took out a ring.

Several in the room began to chuckle and the color in Dinah's cheeks deepened.

Johnsey cleared his throat to quiet the crowd. "I'm glad you could all join us today," he announced. "Want to make this news public. All good news should be." He turned to face Dinah, his voice softening. "You have the best heart of any woman I've ever known, and I'm asking you—no, I'm begging you—to share it with me. I promise to take care of it, to the best of my ability. I will love you till the day I die, Dinah."

Ida swallowed hard at those words, remembering Larson. Just as quickly, she reminded herself that this was a new day, a new opportunity for happiness for Dinah.

"I will care for you and for Carter," Johnsey added, "if you'll have me. Will you, Dinah? Will you marry me?"

Dinah threw her arms around his neck and planted a kiss on each of his cheeks, then uttered a resounding, "Yes!"

Johnsey slipped the ring on her finger and kissed her squarely on the lips. The crowd let forth a roar, along with a round of applause.

Carter raced to his mother's side, jumping up and down. The elderly man who'd entered with Johnsey stood with a smile on his face, watching the scene. Johnsey quickly made the introductions, and everyone was pleased to meet his father at last. Ida found him to be an amiable man, the twinkle in his eye resembling his son's and his smile nearly as broad as his thick mustache.

Just as the crowd thinned, Ida noticed a group coming down the stairs. Her heart seemed to lodge in her throat. Papa led the way, assisting Mick. Intrigue set in as Reverend Langford's smiling face appeared after Mick's. As they moved her way, she heard one thing that stopped her in her tracks.

"Thank you so much for your help, Mr. Mueller." Mick released his hold on one of the crutches and slipped his hand into Papa's for a firm shake.

"Well, son." Mr. Mueller gave him a nod. "How could I turn you down, especially now that the reverend's on board? If he says this is a good idea, it's a good idea. Plain and simple."

Ida's thoughts whirled 'round in her head. Off to her right, her aunt Dinah stood arm in arm with her new fiancé. To her left, the good reverend offered a hand of congratulations to Mick Bradley for building…a gambling hall?

Could the day possibly get any more peculiar?

## Chapter Thirty-Three

Mick did his best to hide a smile as Mr. Mueller crossed the room ahead of him. He sensed Ida's gaze, but didn't look her in the eye, afraid he would give away too much. Instead, he turned his attention to Dinah and Johnsey, asking for a private conversation outside. With Reverend Langford, of course.

After curious glances from Ida, the four headed out to the boardwalk, where Mick gave Johnsey a slap on the back, nearly losing a crutch in the process. He congratulated the happy couple on their engagement.

Then he got down to business. If he could talk the soon-to-be newlyweds into working with him, the final piece to the puzzle would be firmly locked into place.

With anticipation building, Mick turned to Dinah and the questions began.

"Whatever are they doing out there?" Ida paced the floor in front of the register.

Nellie, who had come bounding down the stairs

at the earlier uproar, shrugged. "I haven't got a clue, but if Reverend Langford is involved, it can't be bad."

"I don't know." Ida allowed herself a brief glimpse outside. Mick and Johnsey exchanged a firm handshake, and the reverend looked on with a smile. What shenanigans did they have up their sleeves?

Her question was answered in short order, at least in part. They all entered the store and Dinah cleared her throat, garnering the attention of everyone present.

"We're going to close up shop for a few minutes."

"Excuse me?" Ida gave her a curious look. "In the middle of the day?"

Johnsey nodded. "It's all right. We will return soon. Ida, will you come with us?"

Ida looked back and forth between Mick—whose eyes twinkled merrily—and Dinah, who maintained a straight face. None of this made any sense at all.

Tagging along behind them, Ida made her way out to the boardwalk, half the town of Spring Creek now following. Her heart thumped in anticipation as Mick made his way toward the empty lot.

Sure enough, they stopped directly in front of his property, and he turned to her with a smile on his face. Her heart melted at once, even before he spoke a word.

Mick signaled for her to join him at the front of the crowd. He gently took her hand and gave her a wink. "You're probably wondering what all of this is about."

"I am."

"Well, I don't blame you. But let me put any fears

to rest. I am not now—nor ever, for that matter—building a gambling hall."

A wave of relief flooded Ida's soul. She nodded, doing her best not to cry at the news.

"I wanted to tell you yesterday, but didn't have the chance. I've had an idea brewing for a few days now, one I think—I hope—you will approve of."

"What sort of idea?"

"Let me ask you a question first. What do you think of when you hear the words *German sausage sauerkraut balls?*"

"My kitchen? The workers I feed every day?" Ida said.

He nodded. "And when you hear the words *Wiener schnitzel?*"

Ida couldn't help but smile as she responded. "Something I'm known for around these parts?"

"Yes, you are known for your cooking," he said. "And I knew from the minute I tasted your food that you needed your own place to cook for others."

She stared at the property, absorbing his meaning. "Are you saying…?"

"I'm saying that you're looking at the property for Ida's, the newest restaurant in town, one that's going to rival The Harvey House and any other place that dares to call itself an eating establishment. One that—with all of us pitching in—will turn a nice profit."

A boyish grin spread across his face. "This will be a place the locals and railroad men alike can call their own. What do you think about that, Miss Mueller?"

Ida felt her cheeks warm as she turned to face him with a smile. "Are you serious, Mick? Because if you're teasing me…"

"I can assure you, he is quite serious," Reverend Langford interrupted. "This is a man who refuses to put his boots in the oven."

"I beg your pardon?"

"He's trying to say that I was never meant to be a gambling-hall owner," Mick said. "And that I'm not the man I used to be." As if to prove the point, Mick pointed to his feet. Ida stared at the worn cowboy boots.

"Where in the world did you get those?" she whispered.

"Reverend Langford brought them over. Told me to try 'em on for size. To plant my feet in Texas soil and stay put. So I think I'll do just that."

"A new man needs a new pair of boots," the reverend added, giving Mick a slap on the back.

Mick turned to face Ida and her heart quickened. "There's not a thing about me that's the same," he explained. "I can tell you more about that later, but you've got to trust me when I say that I've crossed over into the Promised Land, and I want you right there with me, by my side." After staring into her eyes for a few seconds, he added, "What do you say?"

"I'm overcome." She shifted her gaze, afraid the tears would come. "The restaurant is a marvelous idea, and I'm so grateful, but…"

"But?"

"But what about the mercantile? Who's going to help Dinah?"

"As quick as she'll marry me, I'll be there," Johnsey said.

"I'll do whatever you need," Sophie called from the back of the crowd. The sight of her best friend overwhelmed Ida as she thought of their recent conversation.

"I'll go on helping, too," Nellie added. "At the mercantile or the restaurant."

"Don't fret, Ida," Dinah encouraged with a smile. "Chase after your dream."

"My dream?" Ida looked at the burned-out lot for a few seconds. She'd always been most comfortable in the kitchen, but how had Mick known? He'd rarely seen her in that role, after all. Did he know her heart even better than she did?

She turned back to him. "I can't do something of this magnitude on my own," she whispered.

He pulled her close. "Exactly. Which is why I'm going to manage the restaurant. I'm going to walk right next to you every step of the way."

"You are?"

"Sure. I've had a few years of experience. In a different field, of course, but still."

The gathered crowd laughed. She looked up into his eyes—warm, loving eyes. Eyes that convinced her this was a man to be trusted. A man who refused to put his boots—new or otherwise—in the oven. Whatever that meant.

Another familiar voice rang out from the back of the crowd. "What's all this I hear about a new restaurant?"

Myrtle Mae.

The older woman pushed her way to the front of the group, and Ida smiled as she noticed her father also standing nearby.

"There you are, girl. Come here and give me a hug," Myrtle Mae said.

After a slight chuckle, Mick released his hold on Ida and she eased her way in Myrtle Mae's direction.

"Now, here's what we're going to do." Myrtle Mae looked at the lot with a wrinkled brow. "Do you think you can handle the breakfast crowd by yourself?"

"With a little help from Nellie, maybe."

"Good girl." Myrtle Mae's voice was all business. "Then I'll take care of the lumber-mill workers until noon. After that I'll come to town to help you. Together we'll whip out some of the best meals folks around these-here parts have ever tasted."

"Are you sure?" Ida could scarcely believe it. To have Myrtle Mae working for her would be an answer to prayer. "But what about your job at The Harvey House? And what about you, Papa? Won't you need her at home?"

"I will come to town for my evening meals," he said. "That way I'll get the best of both worlds."

"And don't let me hear you mentioning The Harvey House again," Myrtle Mae said with a scolding look on her face. "They're our competition now." Ida grinned at Myrtle Mae and thanked her with all her heart.

Ida made her way back to Mick and he wrapped his arms around her, pressing gentle kisses into her hair. She felt him take a deep breath.

"Will you be mine, Ida? Will you take me, broken as I am?"

Ida's heart swelled with joy and she reached up, touching his cheek, whispering, "Broken no more."

# Epilogue

Mick paced the aisle of the church, ready to get the day's events under way. He looked over the congregation, smiling at those who'd come out to offer their support—again. The past couple of months, the townspeople had rushed to help build the new restaurant, offering support of every kind.

He couldn't help but smile as he thought about how happy his bride-to-be looked each morning as she prepared breakfast. How she smiled as folks complimented her favorite dishes. What a success the place had become, and how they'd celebrated together when Mick was able to send his investors their payment in full.

Yes, the good people of Spring Creek were certainly more than friends. They were his staunchest supporters, his prayer partners and his family.

Most of them, anyway. To date, the sheriff hadn't been able to get the necessary witnesses to come forward regarding Mick's attack, but Mick had reconciled himself to that fact. As Ida so often said, "Justice is in the hands of the Lord." He'd wanted to take it into his own hands a time or two, but the Almighty had somehow given him peace in the middle of that storm.

"What do you suppose is taking so long?" he asked the reverend.

His good friend let out a laugh, one that echoed across the crowded room. "Taking so long?" He slapped Mick on the back. "I've performed over thirty weddings and they always run late, even with only one bride involved. But three?" He pulled out his pocket watch and took a look. "I'd say we're doing well if we get this shindig started by one o'clock."

Mick let out a groan. This was supposed to be a noon affair, with a huge meal following. If they didn't get things started—and soon—the flowers would be wilted and the food ruined.

He turned to the two other grooms. From what Mick could tell, Dirk appeared the most anxious. He occasionally pulled out his watch for a cursory glance, but most of his time was spent staring at the double doors in anticipation.

Johnsey remained calm, greeting guests and making small talk. As the minutes ticked by, he eventually made his way up the aisle to the front of the church, where he took a seat next to his father and Emma Gertsch. Interesting, how the two had been spending so much time together.

No, Mick wouldn't think about anyone else's love life today but his own.

And Johnsey's.

And Dirk's.

Now, if they could just locate their brides, they'd have a wedding—one the folks in Spring Creek, Texas, wouldn't soon forget.


"Are you almost ready?"

Ida looked up as she heard Sophie's voice. "Nearly. I'm just trying to get these wayward hairs tucked away." She fidgeted with her up-do, adjusted her veil and pinched her cheeks to give them a rosy appearance. Turning back to her friend, she asked, "How do I look? And be perfectly honest."

"Honestly, Ida. You're the prettiest bride I've ever seen."

Ida took her by the hand. "Bless you for that."

From the back of the room, Myrtle Mae cleared her throat. Loudly. Turning to her, Sophie chuckled then added, "You are an exquisite bride, as well, Myrtle Mae." She then turned her attentions to Dinah, who stood in front of the mirror, fussing with her delicate pearl necklace. With a smile, Sophie said, "Dinah, you are absolutely beautiful in that dress."

Dinah made a graceful turn, showing off the gown that Emma Gertsch had sewn by hand. "I can't believe I actually own a dress I didn't make myself."

"Yes, but look at the great sacrifice on your part. You had to promise Emma a lifetime supply of dime novels in exchange for her work."

Everyone erupted in laughter, and for a moment, all nerves were set aside.

"We are late, ladies. Likely our menfolk are getting anxious," Ida said.

"I don't know about yours," Myrtle Mae said as she moved toward the door of the tiny classroom, "but my man is probably having a fit by now."

"Well, of course he is." Ida drew near and gave her mother-to-be a kiss on the cheek. "This is going to be the happiest day of his life."

"Aw, don't make me cry, Ida." Myrtle Mae glanced in the mirror one last time at her reflection. "I've already done the best I could with what God gave me. I don't want red-rimmed eyes to spoil the effect."

"Nothing could spoil the effect," Dinah added. "You look radiant."

Nellie, who stood nearby holding the bridal bouquets, let out a little sniffle. "This is such a happy day!"

All the ladies gathered together in a hug, smiles on every face. Ida looked at her aunt and Myrtle Mae with a full heart. Together they made their way to the back doors of the church. From inside, Ida heard the familiar strains of the wedding march. Reverend Langford's wife wasn't half-bad on the piano, though Myrtle Mae might disagree. And the dear woman had been practicing for months in preparation for this special day.

"Are you ready?" Dinah whispered, giving Ida's hand a gentle squeeze.

Ida gave a nod and the doors swung wide. Nellie and Sophie—the loveliest of bridesmaids—made their entrance first, fall flowers in hand. Myrtle Mae followed, her wide girth even wider with her full skirt swishing this way and that. Then it was Dinah's turn. She turned to give Ida one last loving glance before heading off to meet her man.

Ida watched it all with hands trembling. Up at the front of the church, she caught her first glimpse of Mick. He stood tall and straight in his suit, crutches no longer necessary. On his feet, as always now, the worn cowboy boots. On his face, an anxious smile.

As their eyes met from across the crowded room, Ida's heart raced in anticipation. She'd no sooner taken her first step toward him than Dinah's words, spoken months earlier, came rushing back at her. '*I predict you will one day look a man directly in the eye—and slapping him will be the furthest thing from your mind.*"

A smile played at the edges of Ida's lips. Yes, she had to conclude. Looking at her Mick from where she now stood, watching the twinkle in those smoky gray eyes, slapping him was indeed the very last thing on her mind.

\* \* \* \* \*

Dear Reader,

In 2004, while eating lunch at Wunsche Brothers Café in Spring, Texas, an idea struck me. Why not write about Texas? Why not share with readers the state I knew and loved? Through the large plate-glass window, I observed a train rumbling by, and another idea took hold. Perhaps I could share what happened to the quaint farming community of Spring in 1902, just after two hundred railroad men moved in and took over.

As you read this "quintessentially Texas" tale, I pray you catch a glimpse of the spirit of the characters. May you also come to fully understand the words that drove Queen Esther when she said "…who knows but that you have come to royal position for such a time as this?" (*Esther* 4:14b).

I love to hear from my readers. You can contact me at booksbyjanice@aol.com. Please visit my Web site at: www.janiceathompson.com.

—Janice Thompson

## QUESTIONS FOR DISCUSSION

1. Ida's town of Spring Creek, Texas, changed when railroad men moved in and took over. Has your town ever changed so dramatically? If so, how did that affect you? How did the Lord help you cope?

2. Ida lost her mother at the tender age of twelve, and at one point feared she might lose her father, too. Have you ever struggled with similar losses or fears? If so, how did you handle them?

3. Mick Bradley comes to Texas with a huge dream. What's the biggest dream you've ever dreamed? Did it come true? Was it God's dream? If so, did you wait for His timing, or move out on your own?

4. Ida admires the biblical character of Esther, and believes she, too, was born "for such a time as this." Have you ever felt like that? Explain.

5. Ida has a tendency to take matters into her own hands. She's a fixer. What about you? Do you try to fix things, too? If so, how has that worked out for you?

6. Mick remembers praying with his mother as a little boy. What about you? Did God begin to woo you as a child? If so, did you walk with Him

from childhood on, or did you go through a straying season?

7. Several times in this story Ida catches Mick and keeps him from falling. In similar fashion, she's trying to keep him from falling spiritually, though she doesn't always go about it the right way. Have you ever tried to keep someone else from falling? What was the result?

8. Johnsey is the best sort of friend—the kind who encourages instead of bringing condemnation, who nudges people toward the Lord in a gentle way. He's there for Mick when he's most needed. Who is the Johnsey in your life? How much do you value this person?

9. Johnsey uses the analogy of the train tracks to tell his story of salvation. Have you ever been on the wrong track? If so, what did the Lord do to turn you around?

10. Carl and Eugene are local young men who are led astray, even though they know better. What about you? Were you raised to know right from wrong, and yet chose wrong at one point in spite of what you knew to be right?

11. Dinah has been through a terrible tragedy in her life, and yet finds love again. Do you know anyone who's been through the valley of the

shadow and experienced a second chance at love? What happened?

12. The reverend in this story has a past. How do you feel about people in ministry having a "sinful past"? Would a sinful past cause you to doubt a spiritual leader's ability to minister, or somehow make you feel he or she was more human?

13. At one point in the story, Mick accuses Ida of being as "unbending" as the railroad tracks. Her stubbornness, at least to his way of thinking, presents a problem. Have you ever struggled with stubbornness? If so, what was the result?

14. Mick is physically crippled, but Ida says, "You're not crippled in the usual way. It's not your bones that haven't mended—it's your heart." She goes on to explain that he needs to make his peace with God. Have you ever been spiritually crippled? How was that "brokenness" mended?

15. In order to reach her "happily ever after," Ida has to let go of a lot of her preconceived notions. What about you? Have your preconceived notions ever gotten in the way of your own happiness? If so, how did the Lord rid you of them?

After weeks in intensive care, police officer Jude Sinclair is finally recovering from the hit-and-run accident that nearly cost him his life. But was it an accident after all? Jude has his doubts—which get stronger when he spots a familiar black car outside his house: the same kind that accelerated before running him down two months ago. Whoever wants him dead hasn't given up, and anyone close to Jude is in danger. Especially Lacey Carmichael, the stubborn, beautiful home-care aide who refuses to leave his side, even if it means following him into danger….

"We don't have time for an argument," Jude said. "Take a look outside. What do you see?"

Lacey looked and shrugged. "The parking lot."

"Can you see your car?"

"Sure. It's parked under the streetlight. Why?"

"See the car to its left?"

"Yeah. It's a black sedan." Her heart skipped a beat as she said the words, and she leaned closer to the glass. "You don't think that's the same car you saw at the house tonight, do you?"

"I don't know, but I'm going to find out."

Lacey scooped up the grilled-cheese sandwich and shoved it into the carryout bag. "Let's go."

He eyed her for a moment, his jaw set, his gaze hot. *"We're* not going anywhere. You are staying here. I am going to talk to the driver of that car."

"I think we've been down this road before and I'm pretty sure we both know where it leads."

"It leads to you getting fired. Stay put until I get back, or forget about having a place of your own for a month." He stood and limped away, not even giving

Lacey a second glance as he crossed the room and headed into the diner's kitchen area.

Probably heading for a back door.

Lacey gave him a one-minute head start and then followed, the hair on the back of her neck standing on end and issuing a warning she couldn't ignore. Danger. It was somewhere close by again, and there was no way she was going to let Jude walk into it alone. If he fired her, so be it. As a matter of fact, if he fired her, it might be for the best. Jude wasn't the kind of client she was used to working for. Sure, there'd been other young men, but none of them had seemed quite as vital or alive as Jude. He didn't seem to need her, and Lacey didn't want to be where she wasn't needed. On the other hand, she'd felt absolutely certain moving to Lynchburg was what God wanted her to do.

"So, which is it, Lord? Right or wrong?" She whispered the words as she slipped into the diner's hot kitchen. A cook glared at her, but she ignored him. Until she knew for sure why God had brought her to Lynchburg, Lacey could only do what she'd been paid to do—make sure Jude was okay.

With that in mind, she crossed the room, heading for the exit and the client that she was sure was going to be a lot more trouble than she'd anticipated when she'd accepted the job.

Jude eased around the corner of the restaurant, the dark alleyway offering him perfect cover as he peered into the parking lot. The car he'd spotted through the window of the restaurant was still parked beside Lacey's. Black. Four door. Honda. It matched the one that had pulled up in front of his house, and the one that had run him down in New York.

He needed to get closer.

A soft sound came from behind him. A rustle of fabric. A sigh of breath. Spring rain and wildflowers carried on the cold night air. Lacey.

Of course.

"I told you that you were going to be fired if you didn't stay where you were."

"Do you know how many times someone has threatened to fire me?"

"Based on what I've seen so far, a lot."

"Some of my clients fire me ten or twenty times a day."

"Then I guess I've got a ways to go." Jude reached back and grabbed her hand, pulling her up beside him.

"Is the car still there?"

"Yeah."

"Let me see." She squeezed in closer, her hair brushing his chin as she jockeyed for a better position.

Jude pulled her up short. Her wrist was warm beneath his hand. For a moment he was back in the restaurant, Lacey's creamy skin peeking out from under her dark sweater, white scars crisscrossing the tender flesh. She'd shoved her sleeve down too quickly for him to get a good look, but the glimpse he'd gotten was enough. There was a lot more to

Lacey than met the eye. A lot she hid behind a quick smile and a quicker wit. She'd been hurt before, and he wouldn't let it happen again. No way was he going to drag her into danger. Not now. Not tomorrow. Not ever. As soon as they got back to the house, he was going to do exactly what he'd threatened—fire her.

"It's not the car." She said it with such authority, Jude stepped from the shadows and took a closer look.

"Why do you say that?"

"The one back at the house had tinted glass. Really dark. With this one, you can see in the back window. Looks like there is a couple sitting in the front seats. Unless you've got two people after you, I don't think that's the same car."

She was right.

Of course she was.

Jude could see inside the car, see the couple in the front seats. If he'd been thinking with his head instead of acting on the anger that had been simmering in his gut for months, he would have seen those things long before now. "You'd make a good detective, Lacey."

"You think so? Maybe I should make a career change. Give up home-care aide for something more dangerous and exciting." She laughed as she pulled away from his hold and stepped out into the parking lot, but there was tension in her shoulders and in the air. As if she sensed the danger that had been stalking Jude, felt it as clearly as Jude did.

"I'm not sure being a detective is as dangerous or as exciting as people think. Most days it's a lot of running into brick walls. Backing up, trying a new direction." He spoke as he led Lacey across the parking lot, his body still humming with adrenaline.

"That sounds like life to me. Running into brick walls, backing up and trying new directions."

"True, but in my job the brick walls happen every other day. In life, they're usually not as frequent." He waited while she got into her car, then closed the door, glancing in the black sedan as he walked past. An elderly woman smiled and waved at him, and Jude waved back, still irritated with himself for the mistake he'd made.

Now that he was closer, it was obvious the two cars he'd seen weren't the same. The one at his place had been sleeker and a little more sporty. Which proved that when a person wanted to see something badly enough, he did.

"That wasn't much of a meal for you. Sorry to cut things short for a false alarm." He glanced at Lacey as he got into the Mustang, and was surprised that her hand was shaking as she shoved the key into the ignition.

He put a hand on her forearm. "Are you okay?"

"Fine."

"For someone who is fine, your hands sure are shaking hard."

"How about we chalk it up to fatigue?"

"How about you admit you were scared?"

"Were? I still am." She started the car, and Jude let his hand fall away from her arm.

"You don't have to be. We're safe. For now."

"It's the 'for now' part that's got me worried. Who's trying to kill you, Jude? Why?"

"If I had the answers to those questions, we wouldn't be sitting here talking about it."

"You don't even have a suspect?"

"Lacey, I've got a dozen suspects. More. Every wife who's ever watched me cart her husband off to jail. Every son who's ever seen me put handcuffs on his dad. Every family member or friend who's sat through a murder trial and watched his loved one get convicted because of the evidence I put together."

"Have you made a list?"

"I've made a hundred lists. None of them have done me any good. Until the person responsible comes calling again, I've got no evidence, no clues and no way to link anyone to the hit and run."

"Maybe he won't come calling again. Maybe the hit and run was an accident, and maybe the sedan we saw outside your house was just someone who got lost and ended up in the wrong place." She sounded like she really wanted to believe it. He should let her. That's what he'd done with his family. Let them believe the hit and run was a fluke thing that had happened and was over. He'd done it to keep them safe. He'd do the opposite to keep Lacey from getting hurt.

\* \* \* \* \*

*Will Jude manage to scare Lacey away, or will he learn that the best way to keep her safe is to keep her close…for as long as they both shall live?*
*To find out, read*
***THE DEFENDER'S DUTY** by Shirlee McCoy*
*Available May 2009*
*from Love Inspired Suspense.*

# REQUEST YOUR FREE BOOKS!

## 2 FREE INSPIRATIONAL NOVELS
## PLUS 2
## FREE
## MYSTERY GIFTS

*Love Inspired.*
# HISTORICAL
### INSPIRATIONAL HISTORICAL ROMANCE

**YES!** Please send me 2 FREE Love Inspired® Historical novels and my 2 FREE mystery gifts (gifts are worth about $10). After receiving them, if I don't wish to receive any more books, I can return the shipping statement marked "cancel". If I don't cancel, I will receive 4 brand-new novels every other month and be billed just $4.24 per book in the U.S. or $4.74 per book in Canada, plus 25¢ shipping and handling per book and applicable taxes, if any*. That's a savings of over 20% off the cover price! I understand that accepting the 2 free books and gifts places me under no obligation to buy anything. I can always return a shipment and cancel at any time. Even if I never buy another book, the two free books and gifts are mine to keep forever. 102 IDN ERYA 302 IDN ERYM

| | | |
|---|---|---|
| Name | (PLEASE PRINT) | |
| Address | | Apt. # |
| City | State/Prov. | Zip/Postal Code |

Signature (if under 18, a parent or guardian must sign)

### Mail to Steeple Hill Reader Service:
**IN U.S.A.:** P.O. Box 1867, Buffalo, NY 14240-1867
**IN CANADA:** P.O. Box 609, Fort Erie, Ontario L2A 5X3

Not valid to current subscribers of Love Inspired Historical books.

**Want to try two free books from another series?**
**Call 1-800-873-8635 or visit www.morefreebooks.com**

\* Terms and prices subject to change without notice. N.Y. residents add applicable sales tax. Canadian residents will be charged applicable provincial taxes and GST. Offer not valid in Quebec. This offer is limited to one order per household. All orders subject to approval. Credit or debit balances in a customer's account(s) may be offset by any other outstanding balance owed by or to the customer. Please allow 4 to 6 weeks for delivery. Offer available while quantities last.

**Your Privacy:** Steeple Hill Books is committed to protecting your privacy. Our Privacy Policy is available online at www.SteepleHill.com or upon request from the Reader Service. From time to time we make our lists of customers available to reputable third parties who may have a product or service of interest to you. If you would prefer we not share your name and address, please check here. ☐

LIH08R

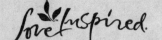
# HISTORICAL

## TITLES AVAILABLE NEXT MONTH

### Available May 12, 2009

**GIFT FROM THE SEA by Anna Schmidt**
The Great War took more from nurse Maggie Hunter than
just her fiancé—it also claimed her faith in God and in
love. Then an injured man washes up on the shores of her
Nantucket home, and to save him, Maggie must learn how to
believe in hope again.

**COURTING THE DOCTOR'S DAUGHTER by Janet Dean**
A dedicated healer working beside her doctor father, widow
and mother Mary Graves has no time for nonsense like
Dr. Luke Jacobs's "elixir of health." But there's more to Luke
than meets the eye. He's got a lifetime of love he's willing to
share, if he can convince Mary to let him into her home, her
family—and her heart.

LIHCNMBPA0409